D1415246

SEAL'S SPITFIRE (SPECIAL FORCES: OPERATION ALPHA)

BLACK EAGLE 1

LYNNE ST. JAMES

SEAL's Spitfire

Dear Readers,

Welcome to the Special Forces: Operation Alpha Fan-Fiction world!

If you are new to this amazing world, in a nutshell the author wrote a story using one or more of my characters in it. Sometimes that character has a major role in the story, and other times they are only mentioned briefly. This is perfectly legal and allowable because they are going through Aces Press to publish the story.

This book is entirely the work of the author who wrote it. While I might have assisted with brainstorming and other ideas about which of my characters to use, I didn't have any part in the process or writing or editing the story.

I'm proud and excited that so many authors loved my characters enough that they wanted to write them into their own story. Thank you for supporting them, and me!

READ ON!
　　Xoxo
　　Susan Stoker

ACKNOWLEDGMENTS

I can't thank Susan Stoker enough for allowing me to "play" with her characters. I love all of her books and being able to incorporate her characters into my stories has been so much fun. Even better, the opportunity to share my books with you is the icing on the cake. Susan is truly special, and I can't express how much I appreciate her friendship and support.

In SEAL's Spitfire, John "Tex" Keegan is part of my story. I have done my best to keep him the same as he is in Susan's books, but I've taken certain allowances for my story.

I really hope you enjoy SEAL's Spitfire. Remember, the best way to thank an author is to leave a review.

Lynne
xoxo

For all the spouses and families who are patiently waiting for their soldiers to come home.

For M.G., because sometimes life gives us donkey balls and there's nothing we can do about it. You will never be forgotten.

As always, for T.S. I love you!

CHAPTER 1

"Attention. Passengers waiting for Delta Flight 363 to Atlanta, your flight will be delayed due to mechanical issues with the plane. Mechanics are currently assessing the issue. As soon as we have more information, we'll advise you. We are sorry for any inconvenience this may cause."

Meghan Henley groaned. She'd gotten to the airport two hours early and now it looked like she was in for a much longer wait. "Dammit all to hell. Inconvenience? No shit. Just fucking perfect," she mumbled mostly under her breath as she rummaged through her purse for her phone. "Stuck in the fucking airport. And they wonder why people have no faith in airlines anymore."

"You wouldn't want to get on a broken plane, would you?"

Startled at the deep voice, she jerked. "Are you talking to me?" she asked as she turned toward the voice. She'd been so focused on her book she hadn't realized someone sat next to her. Let alone 'Mr. Gorgeous' with the dreamy brown eyes.

"Uh huh. Better to be safe than sorry, no?" His voice was smooth like whiskey. He was definitely military—Navy most likely since they were in Norfolk. The patches on his bag gave it away since he wasn't wearing his uniform. God, there was just something about a man in uniform and she could just imagine him in fatigues.

"Yes, of course, it is. I am just looking forward to getting back home. That's all." His voice messed with her insides, but his eyes, damn. She could get lost in those eyes, like jumping into a pool of molten chocolate.

"What?" Heat spread from her neck to her face. She'd been staring while he was talking, and she didn't have a clue what he'd said.

"I said I'm sure we'll be on our way soon enough," he said with a chuckle.

"Yes, probably. Are you headed home too?"

"Not exactly home, but I'm going to visit my sister and my niece and nephew in Denver."

"That sounds like fun."

"Oh yeah. The kids are great. Still young enough to have a lot of fun with their uncle. It'll be good to have some downtime."

"I bet. Navy, right?

"Yes, ma'am. Over ten years now." Calculating numbers in her head, she figured he was probably about thirty depending on when he joined. Not that it mattered, but it was a thing she liked to do—figuring out everything she could about the people she met. It's what made her a good journalist or would if she ever got a chance to really prove herself. Writing obits and stories for the society page wasn't exactly her dream job.

"What about you? Where is home?" She was used to asking questions. It was weird being on the other end.

"My mom lives just outside of Atlanta. I'm going to see her."

"I thought you said you were headed home?" He cocked an eyebrow as he asked the question. His eyebrows were gorgeous. Thick and dark just like his hair. What was wrong with her? She's focusing on his eyebrows? Good God.

"I am, sorta. It was home, now it's not. But I still think of it as home. I have an apartment in DC."

"Now I know where the accent comes from." Accent? She'd worked hard to make it go away while in college. No one had mentioned it in years. How did he hear it?

"I don't..." Before she could finish the intercom sputtered to life.

"Attention passengers on Delta Flight 393 to Atlanta. Due to parts and mechanics being flown in from Atlanta to repair the plane, the flight will be delayed for another few hours." The longer she listened to the message the more her heart sank in

3

her stomach. Getting home tonight was looking less and less possible.

"For your convenience, we can try to book you onto another Delta flight or on another airline. It's possible this flight may be canceled." A collected groan echoed around the waiting area. The group of strangers instantly became comrades in the fight to get out of the airport on a Friday night. Home, vacation, wherever, but everyone wanted out as soon as possible.

"I guess we need to line up with the others..." Meghan mused and glanced at her phone as it pinged with a text message. "Double shit. According to this text, they are canceling the flight."

"Traveling is definitely an adventure," the gravelly voice responded. No southern accent for him, just a low rumble she felt inside.

"Not the adventure I wanted."

"Look around. You're not alone."

"Doesn't this delay bother you?"

"No. It really doesn't. There are so many things worse than being stuck in an airport for a few hours."

"I guess there are. It's just frustrating. Are you going to get on the line to see about another flight?"

"Sure am. Let's see if we can blow this gin joint tonight, shall we?" He was funny on top of being drop-dead sexy. Too bad she hadn't met him in

D.C. Then there was a chance she'd see him again. Still, the view was fine, oh so fine. Wait until she told Lizzie. Now that will be a fun conversation.

As he stood and grabbed his bag, she had to tilt her head all the way back. He was a freakin' giant. "Wow, you're tall." Brilliant, Meghan. The epitome of sophistication. *Wow, you're tall?* WTH was that?

"You think?" He answered with a wide grin. The corners of his eyes even crinkled up. Oh yeah, great impression. She stood and grabbed the handle of her roller bag. The exact opposite of the gorgeous giant, she barely passed the five-foot mark on her tiptoes. She expected after her stellar exclamation that he'd get her back with something.

"Wow. You're short," he said and laughed. "Sorry, I couldn't resist. But it's not a lie."

"No, it's not. You nailed it, big guy."

"Heh. Big guy? We never did get around to exchanging names. Did we?"

"Nope. Not yet." She wanted him to go first. To see if he'd tell her his real name. Not that she'd know for sure, but she'd have a good idea. Just because he was the walking embodiment of a GQ cover and in the military didn't mean he wasn't a psycho. A girl can't be too careful.

"I'm Rafe, it's very nice to meet you," he said as he reached for her hand.

"Meghan. It's nice to meet you too." After hesitating for a moment, she placed her hand in his. She felt so tiny as his hand completely engulfed hers. It was warm and dry. Oh, so warm. And she let him hold on to her for too long.

The color raced back into her cheeks as embarrassment made her cringe inside. She was making a fool of herself in front of a complete stranger. Needing to put some space between them, she grabbed her bag and joined the line. She had to be losing her mind. Never in all of her thirty-two years had she reacted to someone as soon as she'd met them. Lunacy. Pure lunacy.

The line wrapped around the waiting area like a snake. There had to be twenty people in front of them. The queue moved slower than a snail on a turtle. It was going to be a long night. Several of the other passengers were trying to call reservations while they were waiting in line, but she didn't see the point. This was the only available flight to Atlanta that evening. Calling and harassing some person on the other end of the phone wouldn't help anything. A rental car might have been an option if she wasn't so tired.

"I think we're going to be here for a while." Yup his voice was definitely like whiskey as it slid down her throat leaving a trail of heat. Turning to face him, she hoped he'd say something else. It was crazy how attracted to him she was after they just met.

"I agree," she responded. "But like you said, we don't have many options." As she finished her sentence her stomach growled. Ugh. She was batting a thousand, if she could find a way to embarrass herself, she'd get 'er done.

"I'm hungry. How about we grab something to eat after we get our tickets squared away."

She could have kissed him for not saying anything about her tummy sounds. He was earning brownie points left and right. Dinner? With him? Hell yeah, she'd like it. "That's a great idea."

STUCK IN AN AIRPORT on a Friday night was not his idea of fun. But it was a hell of a lot better than where he'd been last weekend. The mission had sucked donkey balls, it had been iffy in the middle, but they'd pulled it off and all made it back home to *not* talk about it. It's all that mattered.

Meeting little Miss Meghan, a tiny bombshell wrapped in spitfire changed everything. And when she answered him in her soft southern drawl he was smitten. Languages were his specialty. He spoke ten fluently and figuring out different dialects and accents was a game. It was also a huge advantage on missions, and he'd already known where home was before she'd said Atlanta. Moving to D.C. must have been recent since there was no trace of it yet.

Not telling him her life story right away told him she was smart, or at least careful. He had a feeling if he hadn't told her his name first, she wouldn't have told him hers. It wasn't enough. She intrigued him and he wanted to know her story, and he'd make it his mission while stuck in the airport to find out. It would make passing the time so much more fun.

"How long does it take to book a new ticket?" The grumbling from other passengers was getting louder the longer it took to figure out what was going on. They still had four passengers in front of them and they'd been on the line for over twenty minutes. It was a tedious process.

"The crowd is getting restless. Be prepared to take cover if food starts flying," Meghan said in a loud whisper. The woman in front of her turned around and gave her a dirty look, and Rafe lost it. She was too funny.

"What?" she asked as she heard his laughter.

"You are funny." He wasn't sure how she'd take it and braced himself for a clever retort, but instead, she shrugged her shoulders and winked while flashing him a devilish smile. She was amazing. Hopefully, she'd give him her number before he lost track of her. Although who knew when he'd be able to get up to DC to see her again.

"Have you been in many food fights?"

"Hell, yeah. Hasn't everyone?"

"No, I don't think so."

"Hmm. They were common occurrences in our house. My baby brother would start them. He was the bad one."

"It sure sounds like it."

"Yeah, that's why it's even funnier that he grew up to be a missionary."

"Seriously?"

"Oh yeah. We still laugh about it and remind him every chance we get."

"And your parents didn't object?"

"Nah. My dad would join in and my mom would just stand in the kitchen shaking her head. But she'd have the last laugh since we had to clean up the mess and the kitchen when we were done."

"She sounds like a great mom."

"She is," Meghan said wistfully. The sadness in her voice triggered his protective instincts and he had to stop himself from pulling her into his arms for a hug. He doubted she'd have appreciated it. Hell, she'd probably have kicked him in the balls for being handsy.

"Do you have your boarding pass?" Finally, it was her turn, and his, with the second gate agent.

"Here you go. I'm supposed to connect to Denver."

"Let me see what we've got available." He looked over and Meghan was going through the same process and getting the same results. Nothing out tonight.

"The earliest open flight to Atlanta is at ten a.m. We won't be able to get you on a connecting flight to Denver until four p.m. tomorrow afternoon."

"That's all you've got?"

"Yes, unless you want to stay on this flight with the hope that they can get it fixed."

"If I do that what's the first flight out of Atlanta to Denver?"

Listening to the clicking of the computer keys, he wondered if it would be better just to rent a car and drive to Atlanta. At this rate, he'd probably get there faster.

"You're kidding, right? Nothing until noon tomorrow?"

Damn, the ten a.m. flight must have booked up while they were standing there. It was looking more and more like he'd just wait it out for this flight. He'd call his sister, she'd understand. He'd already had to postpone this trip three times because he'd gotten spun up.

The gate agent in front of him was waiting for an answer. The first flight to Denver in the morning was nine-thirty a.m. But if he didn't get there he'd have to wait until four or even until Sunday. This was turning into quite the clusterfuck.

"I'll take a chance on this flight but book me onto the first flight to Denver in the morning. I don't want to take the chance it will sell out."

"Of course. Here are your new boarding passes. We are sorry for the inconvenience."

It was an inconvenience, but it wasn't their fault any more than it was his. At least he had a spitfire to take to dinner and she was looking a bit hot under the collar at the moment.

"What did you settle on?"

She looked up at him, her greenish-blue eyes glittering with anger. "Ugh. I'm double booked right now. I decided to take a chance on this flight and booked the first one they had for tomorrow which was noon. It's ridiculous. I know I'm going to spend the night sleeping in one of these chairs."

"I'd say there is a better than a fifty-fifty chance of that. But you won't be alone. I took the same option. I won't get to Denver until either late tomorrow afternoon or Sunday morning though."

"Damn. I'm sorry. I'm complaining, and I only have to get to Atlanta."

"It's okay. Really. You'd be surprised how often this happens."

"I actually considered getting a rental car and driving to Atlanta. But it's getting late and I was worried I'd be too tired."

"I hear you there. I thought about it too. So, still up for some dinner?"

The last meal he'd had was coffee at seven a.m. if you could call that a meal. He'd skipped lunch to get his laundry done. They hadn't gotten back until last night.

She looked up at him with a considering expression. It was his stomach that growled this time and she laughed. Whatever she'd been thinking resolved itself, and she gave him a huge smile.

"Definitely. It sounds like you could eat half a cow."

"You know, I think I could."

CHAPTER 2

It was getting late and the airport was closing but Rafe knew where to find an open restaurant. Meghan was starving and would have eaten a sandwich from a vending machine but sitting down to a huge hamburger and a side of curly fries was nirvana on a plate. When the waitress put her food on the table her mouth watered.

Rafe ordered the same with a beer. She'd have loved a drink but not sure how long she'd be stuck at the airport she was afraid to get a drink and fall asleep. She didn't trust her surroundings enough to go to sleep. Her mom hadn't raised a stupid woman.

Neither spoke while they ate. He devoured his burger in about five bites, but Meghan's eyes were bigger than her stomach as usual. When she pushed her plate away with half of the burger and fries left, she noticed the yearning on Rafe's face.

"Would you like the rest of mine? I'm stuffed."

"You don't want a doggie bag for it?"

"No, I won't be able to eat it and fries are gross when they get cold."

"That's true." He hesitated another few seconds.

"Go ahead, I can tell you want it. Better than letting it go to waste." Without saying a word, he pulled her plate over and inhaled the rest of her meal. She'd never seen anyone eat as fast. It was impressive.

"Better now?"

"Oh yeah. It's my own fault. I haven't eaten anything but coffee since yesterday."

"You consider coffee food?"

"Yeah, don't you?"

"Not sure. A necessity yes, but food? I don't think so. I don't eat the beans or the grounds." Apparently, that was funny because he threw his head back and laughed. Loud enough that it startled the other patrons in the restaurant.

"Sorry, but you are a breath of fresh air."

"I am?" She was just being her usual self as far as she knew.

"Yes, you are. And it's great."

"I'm glad I'm so amusing." She didn't know whether to be embarrassed or annoyed. She didn't usually elicit this reaction from anyone.

"Please don't be offended. I didn't mean anything bad. I just haven't had this much fun with anyone in a long time."

"Okay. If you say so. But I didn't think I'd been funny."

"It's not so much that you're funny, just that you say what you think. Except for my team, it's not what most people do. Women are the worst. Always trying to say what they think you want to hear. The last date I was on, the woman spent the entire night telling me how wonderful I am, how big my muscles are, asking how dangerous my job was, all with the hope of getting into my pants. Sometimes I hate when people figure out I'm in the Navy."

Good thing he couldn't read her mind. She'd been undressing him since they sat down. Wondering if he had a six pack or more under that t-shirt.

"I guess I can accept that. But you know, men do the same thing."

"Touché. But we're usually a lot worse at it."

"Ain't that the truth." Meghan giggled. "Don't you wear regular clothing when you go out? Like today?"

"Yes, but you were able to figure out I was in the service without it. Norfolk is kind of a small town too and we usually hang out in the same places. Makes it easy to know who is military and who isn't."

"So, you can't really blame the women, then can you? If you're in a bar that caters to *your type*, then they know where to go if that's what they want."

"Very true. But sometimes we just want to unwind. Hang out with the guys, shoot some pool, and blow off the remnants of the last mission."

A shadow flitted across his face as he spoke, and her heart squeezed inside her chest. The last mission must have been a doozy. She wanted to ask, but it seemed too much like prying and she had no right to go there. It didn't stop her from reaching across the table and squeezing, or attempting to squeeze, his hand as he held on to his beer mug.

ANOTHER SURPRISE from his little spitfire. She'd gone from defender of women to comforting a stranger in a matter of seconds. It was obvious she'd picked up something from his demeanor. He must be tired normally he hid his emotions better.

"Thank you," he said as he gazed at her small hand over his. It wasn't much larger than his ten-year-old niece's hand.

"You looked sad for a minute."

"I'm really just tired. We got back to base late last night, and I haven't had a lot of sleep lately."

"That sucks…"

He didn't know what if anything she was going to say next because in the space of a heartbeat she was out of her seat and standing in front of the television in the bar.

"Can you turn that up, please?" Her voice sounded strangled in her throat. He put his hand on her shoulder and it was tight as a board. What the hell had just happened. Then he looked up at the screen as the bartender turned up the volume on the TV.

"We've just received word that there has been a bombing in the village of Bamyan. There are several dead and wounded, but we've also learned that a group of missionaries who were there to build a school have been kidnapped. No one has claimed responsibility, but this area is widely known for Taliban infiltrations."

"No, no, no." Meghan's shoulder shook underneath his hand. He doubted she'd even noticed he was touching her.

"Meghan?" He squeezed her shoulder a bit harder. "What's wrong?"

"My brother."

"Brother?"

"Yes." Finally, her focus moved from the screen to him. Her eyes swam with tears and her cheeks were white as chalk. "The Taliban kidnapped my brother."

What were the odds? Pretty shitty obviously. If it was true, then he didn't know how she was still standing at the bar. Not one of the tears spilled out and she hadn't even raised her voice. But she was clearly in shock. He knew the signs way too well.

"C'mon let's go sit down." She didn't answer but

17

didn't fight him when he led her back to their table. The waitress hurried over and he ordered two whiskeys, he needed it and she sure as hell did.

"Here, drink this," Rafe said as he handed her one of the glasses of amber liquid.

"What is it?"

"Scotch. Just take a drink. It will help, I promise." She looked at the glass in her hand like it was some kind of beast but lifted it to her lips and swallowed. If the situation was different, he would have laughed, because as soon as it hit her throat she choked. Not the reaction he'd been going for, but at least it shook her up a bit.

"Holy crap..." Meghan's voice was raspy from coughing. But she was back with him.

"Sorry, but you needed something. You were going into shock."

"I was? Yeah, I suppose I was. Thank you. I think."

"You're welcome. Now, how about you tell me what's going on? And why you think the Taliban kidnapped your brother?"

Rafe wasn't sure she'd heard his question. Maybe the scotch hadn't shaken her up enough. Then she lifted the glass to her lips and took a tentative second drink. No coughing this time, and she no longer looked like a corpse. It also meant she was thinking not just functioning. He'd give her as much time as she needed but patience wasn't one of his virtues and one that his boss, Jake, constantly ripped him about. It wasn't like they were getting out of there anytime soon. There was no rush, but damn he wanted answers.

"My brother is in Afghanistan with his missionary group." His stomach twisted, he didn't need to hear her words to know what was coming next. Fuck.

"They raised money and went there to help rebuild a school that had been destroyed. It has to be his group."

"It's possible it is, but there could be other groups there," Rafe responded. It was his turn to reach across the table to comfort her. When he touched her hand, it was ice cold and sent a shiver down his spine.

"I don't think so. I mean yes, there are others. But I'm almost positive that the village they said is the one he's in. I need to call my family. I need to find out what we can do." As she rummaged through her purse for her phone, he thought about calling Jake to see if they could get any intel at least for her. But that would be pushing it. Nope, not Jake but he knew someone else he could call who worked outside the boxes.

"What are you going to say to them?"

"I don't know. I'm calling my sister. I don't think my mom can deal with this." Before she had a chance to make her call, her phone rang. He'd bet it was the sister but prayed it was the brother saying he was okay.

"Lizzie. Damn. You saw it too? I'm stuck in the airport. It's a long story. Does mom know? Good. Try to keep it that way until I get there. We'll get him back if I have to go there myself to kick some Taliban ass. Okay. Love you too. Big hugs to the kids. I'll be there as soon as I can."

Fresh tears filled her eyes as she disconnected the phone. He had to fight the urge to take her into his arms. If there was anyone in need of a hug, it was her. But they'd only met three or four hours ago. The last thing he wanted to do was overstep a boundary. Fuck it. If she freaked out, he'd deal with the fallout, but she needed a hug in the worst way, and he needed to give her one.

He doubted she noticed he'd gotten out of his chair since she was sitting there staring at her phone screen. Probably trying to figure out what to do next. But there wasn't anything she could do. Not as a civilian. She could call her congressman, but on a Friday night, she'd just get an answering machine. The state department would take a message and call her back. There truly was nothing she could do. But he could and would do something.

Grabbing her hand, he lifted her out of her chair and wrapped her in a big bear hug. He didn't squeeze her tight at first, waiting for her initial reaction. He was prepared to step back and protect the jewels if necessary.

Small arms slipped around his waist and she

snuggled into his chest. Thank God he'd read her right. He pulled her in a little closer until she was closed in the cocoon of his arms.

"Thank you." Her voice was muffled against his chest, but he heard it and felt the vibration.

"You're very welcome. Any better?"

"Yes, but if it's okay with you I'll just stay here for a minute or so more."

"I'll stand here until the plane leaves if it will help."

"I'm afraid you can't do that," the waitress said as she dropped their bill on the table. "We're closing now. I'm sorry."

Meghan pulled out of his arms so quickly she would have fallen if he hadn't grabbed her arm. "Easy there, Spitfire."

"What did you call me?"

"Uhhh. Spitfire. It's a plane."

"I know what it is, but why... Oh never mind. I'm sorry if we kept you late." Meghan reached for her purse he presumed to get her wallet. Since he'd eaten most of their meals there was no way he would let her pay for her dinner.

"I've got it," Rafe said as he handed the waitress his debit card.

"You don't have to."

"I know I don't, but I ate more of your dinner than you did." She seemed to think about it and then nodded.

"Thank you for dinner, and the company."

"Again, you're welcome. But I'm not going anywhere," he answered as he looked at his watch. "At least not for the next four hours if the text I got from Delta is right."

"Four hours? Better than canceled, I guess. I need to get to Atlanta. My family needs me." He'd expected her to be having a hissy fit or whining, crying, something, but she lived up to his view of her. She'd break down eventually, but it wouldn't be in public among strangers. Right now, her mind was going a million miles a minute working on the problem. He knew it for sure because that's what he'd have done.

CHAPTER 3

Four more hours of sitting there doing nothing was going to make her crazy. Pacing wouldn't help. It was after ten p.m. on the east coast, if she could even get someone in the state department, they wouldn't do anything right now. Just a bunch of missionaries. These things happened all the time, that's what they'd tell her. Charlie knew he was taking a risk, but it was his mission. He believed God would watch over them.

"You'd better not let him down either," she mumbled as she sat down in the waiting area once again. These had to be the most uncomfortable seats on the planet.

"I'm not sure what you mean?" Rafe commented from beside her.

"Sorry. I didn't mean to say that out loud. I was thinking about Charlie. My brother. It was something he said before he left."

"Gotcha. I'm a good listener if you want to talk about it."

"Thanks. I appreciate the offer. I'm antsy, I need to do something. Sitting here like a bump on a log is going to drive me out of my fucking mind." Damn. Even she heard the accent that time. Stress, baby. It had been erased by her mini-Virginia vacation with her best friend. But now she had it back, in spades.

The few days hanging out with Chrissy had been great and she'd been so relaxed, ready to tackle her editor to get better assignments. Chrissy was always so good for her. Pushed her to be the best she could be. It had been the first time they'd gotten together since she'd gotten a job for the FBI at Langley. She was one smart cookie and they were lucky to have her analyst skills.

"I understand. It sucks when your hands are tied, and you have to wait on others for answers. Although, I'm not sure how soon you'll get any since it's the weekend."

"I know. It's part of what's making me crazy. There's got to be a way to find out something, anything."

Rafe had a strange expression. It wasn't one she'd seen before and she'd cataloged a bunch of them in the time they've spent together. This was almost like guilt. But what could he feel guilty over? It's not like he could jump on his ship and race over there in a week and rescue Charlie.

"Hopefully you'll hear some good news while we're waiting."

That made her laugh. This whole return trip had been a big ole hot mess. If she'd been smart, she'd have called Chrissy the moment the flight was canceled and stayed with her. But on the other hand, she wouldn't have met the giant hunk of sexiness sitting next to her, but he was only a temporary distraction.

"You're in the Navy. What do you think will happen to them? The missionaries?"

"I don't know. The Taliban, if it is really who took them, will probably want a ransom." That's what she thought too, but was he saying that to reassure her or was it what he believed?

"Is it horrible to hope it's the Taliban and not ISIS? I don't think they'd have a hope in hell if it's them." Rafe didn't answer, but the anger in his eyes was enough. It made her wonder what he did in the Navy. He never said but then she hadn't asked. He didn't know what she did either. They were still just strangers.

She'd wanted a distraction. She got one and should have known better than to even think what else could happen. The universe always had a way of showing you.

"Attention passengers on Delta Flight 393. I'm sorry to say it looks like it will be morning before we can take off. We have hotel room vouchers for anyone who wants one."

It was tempting to get a room, lie down and get a few hours of sleep. But not tempting enough. She wouldn't sleep, she'd just pace and wring her hands, and go online searching for anything she could dig up. In other words, she'd drive herself out of her mind. So no, she'd stay put right where she was and hope that they'd get the damn plane fixed before morning.

"Are you going to take the voucher?"

"Nope. I have an apartment, I could just go there. But they closed security about an hour ago. If anyone leaves, they can't get back in until five a.m."

"They should tell people that."

"Probably, but I don't think they care if they're getting a room."

She turned her head toward the gate agent's desk where a queue had formed. He was right, everyone looked like they were ready to pack it in. Some of them had been there as long as she had, which after checking her watch was just over seven hours. Way too long to spend in an airport.

"Good point. So basically, we're stranded in here, nothing is open for food, no way back in if we go out. Makes me glad I don't smoke, I'd be up a creek without a paddle."

Rafe chuckled. "Too true. And I wouldn't want to see that either. People get mean when they can't smoke."

"I take it you've had some experience with that?"

"My dad. He had a heart attack a few years ago and they made him give up smoking. He wasn't fun to be around. I really felt for my mom."

"It's good you didn't pick up the habit."

"Yes, it is. I'd have never made it this far if I smoked."

"I've been wondering. Just what do you do in the Navy? Are you on a ship? You mentioned missions."

"I'm a frogman, also known as a Navy SEAL."

"Holy shit. For real?" Way to go, Meghan. It's great that you're using your grown-up words.

"Yes, for real," he said as he continued to chuckle. She was sure her expression was comical. But her emotions were all over the place, so she could be forgiven for her doofiness, right?

"I'm sorry."

"You have absolutely nothing to be sorry about."

"Thank you. This is probably way out of line, but is there anything you can do to find out about Charlie?"

RAFE EXPECTED her question as soon as she found out he was a SEAL. And who would blame her? His Spitfire was scared and desperate to save her brother. In her shoes, he'd have done the same thing. What he couldn't do is help. Not officially. As much as it killed him to say no, he had no choice.

But he could call his secret weapon, Tex, a medically retired SEAL who was a computer genius. If there was information out there, he could find it and had pulled their asses out of the fire more times than he cared to remember. Tex had to stay his secret, at least for now.

"I wish I could. But it doesn't work that way."

"You can't fault a girl for trying, right?" The tiny ray of hope on her face dimmed so quickly he wasn't sure it had been there.

"Not at all. Believe me, if there was anything I could do I would." Rafe hated lying to Meghan but he wasn't even sure what Tex could find. It wasn't a military operation. The man was a miracle worker but there was always the first time he'd strike out. To make promises to help and then not be able to come through was worse than lying.

"It's okay. I'm just grasping at straws. I told him he shouldn't go. But he's so damn stubborn."

Rafe smiled gently and draped his arm along the chair behind her. She leaned against him and his smile grew a bit bigger. He didn't think she even realized she'd done it.

"How long has he been a missionary?"

"Five or six years now. Well, doing this type of stuff. He went to college and then worked in local neighborhoods around Atlanta trying to help. Then he heard about this group, Deliver Hope Ministries, and before we knew it, he was flying off to Africa. He was there for a couple of years, then they went to the next place."

"He sounds like a great guy."

"Oh, he is. A stubborn little shit, but he'd give you the shirt off his back."

"And how long has he been in Afghanistan?" He hated pumping her for information about her brother, but the more he could share with Tex the better chance he had of finding something.

"About six months. I think…" Whatever was coming next was cut off by the ringing of her phone. "Sorry, it's my sister. I need to take this."

"Go ahead. I'll give you some privacy." It was the perfect opportunity to give Tex a call without arousing her suspicion. If she hadn't been so distracted about everything she probably wouldn't have shared as much. There was still a lot he didn't know.

Rafe strolled over to the windows and gazed out into the night sky. The airport was quiet, the only people still there were waiting at their gate. What had started out as an overfull plane was down to about fifteen people. Most of them were stretched out on the floor with red Delta Airlines blankets. Not wanting to be overheard, he made sure he was far enough away to have privacy for the call.

As he scrolled through his contacts looking for Tex's number, he realized it was after twelve. In the old days it wouldn't have been bad but now he had a wife and two kids. Maybe he should leave it until morning. Then he glanced toward Meghan and caught her wiping tears she'd managed to hold back for hours.

It sealed the deal. They could get clearance on the plane at any time now and then she'd be out of his life. This was his chance to help. With his decision made, he clicked on Tex's number and waited for it to ring.

"Rafe? What's up?"

"Hey, Tex. Sorry, it's so late."

"It's not that late. I'm assuming this isn't a social call?"

"No, it's not. I'm not even sure you can help. Did you happen to see the news about the missionary group kidnapped in Afghanistan today?"

"Yeah. Are you being sent out?" No one was supposed to know about their missions, but there wasn't much they could keep from Tex if he wanted to know.

"Not this time, at least not so far. I'm stuck in Norfolk Airport and I met a woman."

"You called me at midnight to run a background check?"

"Asshole. I never even considered that. But it's not like that. Okay, it might be, but dammit you're distracting me."

"She must be something to put you off your game."

"That's neither here nor there. Her brother was one of the missionaries kidnapped and she's beside herself. And before you ask, no I haven't told her about you."

"I know better than that. I'm only giving you shit. What info do you have for me?" After that, it was all business. As Rafe told him all he knew about Charles Henley, he heard the tapping of the computer keys on the other end.

"That's all I've got. Hopefully, it's enough to find out something."

"I'll do what I can. What time is your flight?"

"No fucking clue. It was supposed to be four-forty-five yesterday. Now we're waiting to hear if they can fix it. If not, I'm out of here on a ten a.m. flight."

"And the sister?"

"Meghan. She's stuck here until the later flight in the afternoon. Not sure what time."

"Okay, I'll get to work and hit you back when I've got something."

"Thanks, Tex. Say hi and apologize to Melody for me for interrupting your evening."

"Will do." Rafe hoped that Tex could work some magic for Meghan.

CHAPTER 4

"Hi Lizzie, everything okay?" Meghan asked as she smiled at Rafe as he got up to give her some privacy.

"Yes, no. I don't know. I'm at my wit's end. I can't turn on the TV in case they mention something about Charlie. I brought Mom over here because I was worried about her seeing something that would freak her out. She is still lucid more than not."

"I know. Which is good and bad at the moment. I'm not ready to lose her or Charlie. But until we know more information, I don't think we should tell her about it."

"I agree. When are you getting in? It will be a lot easier when I'm not dealing with this alone."

"I'm not sure. Possibly in the middle of the night if they get this plane off the ground. Or not until around two p.m."

"Sweet Jesus. What kind of an airport are they running over there? And why aren't you staying with Chrissy?"

"I wanted to try to get on the delayed flight. If I left, I wouldn't be able to get back in until morning."

"That makes sense sort of. Have you heard anything? Any updates?"

"No, nothing. The TV monitors are on CNN, but I haven't heard any updates about it."

"Damn. I keep hoping we're wrong. That this is a terrible mistake."

"Me too. But my gut says otherwise. When is Craig getting home?"

"Not until Tuesday. He's stuck in San Francisco for the conference. Timing sucks as usual, but he's up for a promotion."

"But that's good news. Right? And I'll be there tomorrow at the latest. If I have to, I'll rent a car and drive there."

"Right. I'm sorry. I'm really not losing it. Okay, maybe I'm losing it a little. We'll be fine until you get here."

"I know you will. Love you, Lizzie."

"Love you too, Meggy."

"Ugh, don't call me that or I'll stay in Norfolk."

"Bye." As she disconnected the call, she felt a bit better. She'd made her sister laugh and no news was good news. Home was under control with her sister holding down the fort. So now it was just figuring out what she could do. There had to be something instead of just sitting there.

"How are things with your sister?" He'd surprised Meghan again. Damn the man had stealthy moves. Duh, SEAL.

"Hanging on as best she can while dealing with her two kids and our mom."

"Is your mom sick?"

"No, yes, not in a regular way. She has Alzheimer's but it's early yet and she's still able to live at home alone. We have someone come in daily to help her around the house but she's still pretty self-sufficient."

"What did your sister call you that you hate?"

"Oh no. You don't get to know that. It's horrible. I prefer Spitfire," Meghan said while rolling her eyes.

"You got it. I kind of like it myself." He smiled showing off his bright white teeth as he said that, and she couldn't resist smiling in return. He'd kept her sane. A total stranger, but he didn't feel like a stranger. Maybe being stuck in the same situation changed the way people interacted. There was probably a study about it somewhere.

"I wish we'd hear something."

"About the plane or your brother?"

"Either, both, just something. This waiting is driving me fucking bonkers."

"I have a question for you. I know we just met tonight, but would you consider giving me your cell number? I'd really like to keep in touch. And see you when I can get up to DC."

When he said he had a question, asking for her number was the last thing she'd expected. Why that would be a surprise after the way the rest of the day was going, she had no idea. For the last two hours, she'd talked about Charlie and nibbled on her thumbnail until her finger was sore.

"You want my number?" Isn't that what he just asked? If he was trying to distract her, he was doing a great job. "Sure, I guess so. I mean why not? Realistically I'll probably never hear from you again."

"I wouldn't say that, but you won't know until you give me a chance."

"Okay, it's two oh two, five five five, five four five three."

"Thank you, Meghan. Would you like mine?" Well duh. Not that she'd ever call him. But still, he was the sexiest man she'd ever seen, considerate, funny, everything she'd dreamed of for a forever. But the timing sucked donkey balls. It was the story of her life.

"Sure." She took out her phone, opened up the contact screen, and then typed in his name and entered the numbers as he gave them to her. She was proud of herself when she remembered to click on "save" before she closed the screen.

"You can call me anytime. If I don't answer, I'm on a mission and I'll call you back as soon as I'm able. I promise." Yeah, he was as perfect as perfect could get. Mom would love him. But he was pain just waiting to happen. Men in his line of work didn't settle down and she wasn't looking for drive-by dates. Why was she thinking about it when she should be trying to figure out how to help Charlie?

"You're doing fine. I know you're worried about your brother. Think about it though, you don't know for sure he is even in trouble. Take a deep breath and try to relax. If the bar was still open, I'd buy you another drink. But instead, you're stuck with my sparkling conversation."

Sparkling conversation? Oh yeah, she'd take that for as long as she could get it. After she got to Atlanta, sparkling anything would be the furthest thing from her mind. Rafe was a good distraction, and he was going all in on keeping her mind entertained and off thoughts of Charlie.

He told her about his team, talking about them like they were his family. Considering what was expected of them she could see why. They were probably closer than most real brothers. As she listened to his descriptions of his team, they materialized in front of her. The detail he painted was like seeing a picture that came to life. It was incredible.

"You should write."

"Letters?"

"No, I mean books."

"I don't think so. It's not me. I like reading but writing? Nope. No patience for that."

"It's a shame. I think you'd sell a ton of books."

"I'd never write about what I do. It's classified and changing the names or locations isn't enough for me."

"I understand. I write. Sort of. It's my job. I went to school to be a journalist, to travel the world and report. Instead, I'm stuck sitting at a desk. All I get to do is write obituaries and stories about the latest socialite scandal."

"You could always do your own blog or something. Set up a site and monetize it."

"It's not that easy, and I need my salary to pay the bills. I have been doing this for almost five years. My break has to come sometime."

"It will."

"What makes you so sure of that?"

"Because they'd be crazy not to give you a chance. I've seen how you scope out your surroundings. I bet I could ask you what anyone in this area was wearing and you'd be able to tell me."

The color crept up her neck. Of course, he'd have noticed that. He'd done the same thing. "I'm not the only one."

"I didn't say you were. But it's a good skill. For writing and it could save your life one day. You never know. But it goes back to covering stories. That will be a huge asset for you when you get your break."

"From your mouth to God's ears," Meghan replied with a sigh. Rafe squeezed her shoulder and she'd forgotten she'd been leaning against him while they'd been talking.

"Chin up, Spitfire. It will happen." The nickname brought a grin to her face. When she met his eyes, he returned her grin. There was something different in his eyes this time, but before she could analyze it another announcement started.

"Attention passengers for Delta Flight 393. The repairs have been completed and your crew is on their way. We should be departing within the hour." Before Jan the gate agent finished her announcement, they'd started cheering. The flight would be mostly empty since there were only about ten of the original passengers out of two hundred still waiting.

It was fine with Meghan. If Rafe didn't sit with her, she'd be happy to stretch out across a row and try to get a little shut-eye. It felt like days since she'd slept.

THE COLLECTED RELIEF felt at the gate was tangible. Rafe joined in that relief. They'd be taking off about three a.m. and it meant he'd be able to catch the early flight to Denver and be with his family by noon or one their time. Now he just hoped that Tex would have something for him before he said goodbye to Meghan.

"Thank God. I was starting to think I'd have to have one of these seats named after me," Meghan said.

"We could still do it if you want. I'm game. We can write our names on the bottom of the seats."

The look she gave him was priceless. Her lips formed into a huge "o." "No way, you're going to deface private property? What would your team-mates say?" Her indignance cracked him up.

Smacking him in the chest, she said with a laugh, "Dang it. I should have known better, huh?"

"Ouch. You've got an arm on you." It had been nothing, well not nothing. Her touch sent heat radiating across his chest. If just her slight touch could do that, he'd love to know what having her naked body against him would feel like.

"Riiiighhhhttttt. And I've got a bridge I can sell you too."

"Want to sit with me on the plane? Or would you rather try to get some rest? I know you're walking into a shitshow when you get home." He'd surprised her again. She must not have much expe-rience with good men. He'd never even asked if she had a boyfriend or a husband. No ring on her finger didn't mean much these days. He'd just assumed she was available. Bad on him.

"Do you think we'll be able to sit where we want?"

Rafe looked around at the sleepy group, he couldn't imagine that the flight attendants would care where they sat as long as they weren't trouble. They'd been waiting around too and were probably exhausted. "I would think so. I guess we'll find out soon. Looks like they are getting ready to board."

"I know I'm not supposed to, but can I leave my bag with you while I uhh run to the ladies' room?"

"Of course. I'll protect it with my life."

"No doubt," she said as she got up and walked away while still smiling. He loved making her smile and her laugh was contagious. It also gave him a chance to check his phone for messages from Tex. His pocket had vibrated a few times, but he didn't want to check in front of Meghan.

Tex had been busy. He had four messages all from him. Scrolling through, he was surprised how much he'd managed to dig up in just a few hours. But he did get verification that it was Meghan's brother's group.

Replying with a few more questions and an update on his own status, he tucked the phone away before she returned but not by much. Other than the dark circles under her eyes, you'd never know she'd spent most of a day in the airport. Tiny, yes, but she wasn't some half-starved waif. Her curves were in all the right places and made him itch to hold her again. It had been heaven to have her in his embrace for even a few moments.

If you'd asked him what his "type" was he

41

wouldn't have an answer. He didn't really date, rarely saw a woman more than one or two times. His free time was valuable to him and he'd rather spend it with the guys or alone. Then he met Meghan. She was so different from any of the women he'd met, more like his sister but not really either.

There was no pretense about her. Like his sister, Dawn, what you saw is what you got. But Meghan was a lot to get. Her black hair fell in sheets around her shoulders, so dark it was like looking at a moonless sky in the desert. Pale skin told him she rarely got outside and worked too much. Her hazel eyes were the most expressive he'd ever seen. He wondered if she realized everything she was feeling, and thinking was visible in the blue-green depths.

Did he want to dull the smile that she wore as she approached him? Bringing up the news about her brother would rip it off her face faster than he could get the words out. She'd asked him to get information if possible. Would telling her now do anything to help, or just make the plane ride a living hell?

"I feel better. I apologize if my breath was a bear. My mother would have had my hide for chatting without brushing after dinner."

"You're fine. I swear and if I meet your mom, I promise not to tell her." Feeling the lightness of her mood helped him make the decision. He'd hold on to his information until they got to Atlanta. She deserved a respite no matter how short.

"Thank you. I appreciate that," she answered with a wink. Yup, holding off was definitely the right thing to do.

CHAPTER 5

The flight went without a hitch. All the passengers were not only allowed to sit where they chose but encouraged to sit in First Class. It somehow made the entire ordeal a little easier to swallow and the free drinks didn't hurt either.

Meghan and Rafe chatted throughout the flight in hushed tones to not disturb the other passengers. There was something about talking in the near darkness that made it easier to share the deepest private thoughts. Sharing her greatest fear —disappointing her mother—was huge. She'd never told anyone, not even Chrissy. Her mom had always believed in her children and encouraged them to follow their dreams. But what she was doing now wasn't even close to living her dreams. How had she let it go on for so long? Five years in a dead end job was too much.

Thinking about it, she shivered, as acid roiled in

her stomach. Maybe the vodka and tonic hadn't been a good idea.

"Are you cold? I can get you another blanket."

"No, I'm fine. Thanks. Just a ghost walking over my grave." She was surprised that even in the dim light he noticed the movement.

"A what?"

"You've never heard that expression?"

"Can't say that I have."

"It's the feeling you get when something is odd, makes you shiver or gives you the weird feeling in your tummy. Makes your hair stand up and goose-bumps pop out."

"Ah yes. When I get that it usually means a shit show is about to break out. Not pretty."

"I'd say not."

"So, what are you worrying about?"

"I was thinking about my brother. He's living his dream but now it may take his life."

Rafe nodded and averted his eyes. Did he know something? Had he heard something? He said he couldn't look into it, but what if he had? What if he already had bad news for her? Panic started to set in, her lungs weren't working, she tried to inhale, but no air filled her lungs. Sweat dotted her forehead, and she grabbed her chest, trying to make her lungs work. Terrified she was going to suffocate, she bent at the waist and hoped it would help.

Rafe must have seen her distress and he pulled her into his lap. With his large hands on either side of her face, he made sure she was looking at him. "Spitfire, focus. Breathe in, slowly. Now breathe out. Slowly. Put your hands on my chest and follow my lead."

Slowly her panic eased, she wasn't going to die. In and out, taking each breath with Rafe.

"There you go. Feel better?"

"A little. Thank you. I was… I couldn't breathe, I thought I was going to die."

"Do you have panic attacks often?"

"Is that what it was? Then no. This is the first and I hope to God my last. I don't think I could take another one."

Rafe smiled gently. "I don't blame you. I've never had one, but I've witnessed way too many."

"I guess I have an overactive imagination. When you looked away when we were talking about Charlie it made me think you knew something. Something horrible…"

Rafe's eyebrows lifted in surprise. "You are extremely observant."

"Yes, we've discussed this. Remember? You're stalling. It means you do know something. You have to tell me, whatever it is." It's also when she realized she was sitting in his lap. She didn't remember how she got there but it wasn't a bad place to be. Did she want to stay there depending on what he had to say? She couldn't decide if she was mad at him or not for holding back informa-tion. From the little he'd said, and what she surmised from her observations, he was all about comfort and help. Getting mad at him for trying to protect her wasn't really fair but neither was hiding information about Charlie.

Rafe pulled his hands away from her shoulders where they'd moved to as she calmed down. She wanted to tell him to keep them there, but she didn't. She would be brave no matter what he had to say. It was time to move back to her seat, as comforting as her present location was, she needed some distance.

"I'm sorry. My intention was to tell you when we landed. You were finally relaxed. I thought you needed some down time before you walked into the Lion's Den at home."

"It wasn't your right…"

"I know. But it's not official information either. It's from an exceptionally talented friend who knows his way around computers like most people know the alphabet."

"Please, just spit it out. I need to know. Is he dead?"

"No. At least we don't think so. But you were right, his group has been kidnapped. As of zero two thirty, no ransom demand had been made."

"Thank God. Why wouldn't you tell me that? It's good news."

"Good? I figured getting confirmation that he had been kidnapped would be devastating. Until then you still could hold on to the hope that it hadn't been him."

"Maybe, but that's not how my mind works. To me knowing is half the battle. Now I need to formulate a plan to get him back. Get them all back."

"Wait. You are a civilian. You can't just go over there on a one-woman rescue mission. You have to leave it to the people who do this for a living. People like me."

"Really? What are the odds they'll send you for a bunch of missionaries? ISIS and the Taliban have killed how many people? How many people are rescued if they're not deemed important by the government?" It wasn't fair, and definitely not something he could control but it felt good to be angry instead of devastated.

"Shhh, you'll wake the others. I understand how upset you are. I do."

"How could you know? Has someone in your family been kidnapped?" She was definitely being unfair, and her voice got louder as her anger escalated. Was this a reverse panic attack? These mood swings were not normal for her.

"Meghan. Stop for a moment. Take a breath. Listen, this is part of being in shock." It seemed like as good a reason as any. She was definitely acting out of character. It was her role to be the calm one, the one who handled all the family problems and emergencies. He was right, she needed to pull herself together. Walking into her sister's house like this would be a disaster because as soon as the door closed behind her, she'd be bombarded.

"I'm sorry. I didn't mean it. Well, some of it."

"I know," Rafe answered and smiled gently. "I shouldn't have kept the information to myself. But even thinking about going to Afghanistan by yourself is a horrible idea." Yeah, he was trying to be nice. She'd expected him to say it would be crazy. That she was out of her mind.

"Maybe. But I can't sit home and do nothing."

"Call the state department. Or actually, they may have called your mother already. She'd be the logical contact unless your brother is married?"

"No, he's not married. And my mom is at my sister's house for now."

"Check her messages, I'm not sure how they operate. They might have called your sister too."

"Right. I hadn't thought of that. Seriously though, if you were in my position, what would you do?" She half-expected him to blow off the question. It sounded silly to her too. He's a Navy SEAL and she's a civilian reporter who'd never been out of the country. How could you compare them?

"Honestly, I don't know. But my boss wouldn't let me go over there for a rescue mission either. Not on my own. I have more rules to follow than you do."

Another thing she hadn't thought through. Of

course, he did. The military was nothing but rules and as an elite team, they probably had extra since all of their missions were classified.

The announcement came to prepare for landing. Meghan wasn't sure if she was happy or not. Exhausted, stressed, and definitely on edge. In another half hour, she'd be saying goodbye to Rafe, probably forever. It was nice that he'd asked for her number, but she never expected him to use it. Whether she'd call him was highly unlikely as well. She was just another woman at another stop in his life.

As if reading her mind, he put his hand over hers on the armrest. "Meghan, there is one thing I want you to hold onto about your brother. If being a missionary is truly his dream, then he won't have regrets. I can guarantee that. He'll feel bad about leaving his family, but if the worse happens, he'll leave this life having followed his chosen path. We have to deal with that too. Every mission could be our last, but it's what we chose, our life's work, our passion."

Once again, Rafe was right. If the worst thing happened and Charlie didn't come home alive, he'd lived his life on his own terms. Now, it was time to start living her life and chase her dreams.

THANK FUCK his team wasn't with him. His reputation as the woman whisperer would go right out the window and he'd never live it down. Instead, he'd made a colossal fuck-up. And even worse, he didn't know if she'd forgive him. All he'd wanted to do was help her. Instead, he overstepped and tried to protect her. That right had to be earned, to be given, not just taken.

She hadn't pulled her hand away. But she was staring out the window, and he could only see her profile. The muscle was ticking in her jaw. He didn't know if she was just pissed-off, concentrating, or something else. She knocked him off balance and was living up to the nickname he'd given her.

Time was running out for them. Once they landed and taxied to the gate, she'd walk away. He had her number, but if he couldn't repair the rift he'd just made, he was doubtful she'd answer his calls. She'd wormed her way into his heart like no other woman he'd met. If it took moving heaven and earth to get her brother back, he would. He'd do anything he could to put a smile back on his little spitfire's face.

"Meghan?"

"Huh, yeah?"

"I'm really sorry I didn't tell you right away. I hope you can forgive me." She turned from staring out the window and met his eyes. The cabin lights had come on and he could see the determination gazing back at him.

"You are a protector, Rafe. It's in your genes. You did what you thought was best. How could I not forgive you?" Could it be that easy?

"Thank you." He meant it with all his heart. This tiny woman had changed his life in a span of eight hours. Watching her walk away would be the hardest thing he'd ever done. But he had to let her go, at least for now. But whether she knew it or not, she was going to be his. "I'll let you know if my friend comes up with anything else."

"Thank you." He saw the truth of her words in her eyes and relief washed over him.

"Just promise me you won't do anything without talking to me first. If there is any way or anything I can do to help I will."

"I appreciate that, but you don't have to. You have your own life."

"Don't you feel it? This thing between us? I can't – no won't let you just walk out of my life."

Surprise and something else flashed in her eyes before she looked away. Whatever was there she didn't want him to see it, to read her. But it was too late. He saw it, and he'd hold on to it until his dying breath.

"Meghan?"

"You... I... we just met. This can't be real. Like you said, I'm in shock. And you're a protector. It's not real."

"It's very real, sweetheart, whether you want to admit it or not."

53

"Love at first sight only happens in cheesy romance novels. Not real life."

"Whether you believe it or not. I do. I might not have yesterday but today proved it to me. You call me a protector? You're right, except now I'm yours."

Before she answered the plane touched down on the runway at Atlanta-Hartsfield Airport. Yesterday he would have been celebrating. Today he was dreading the opening of the airplane door.

As the plane taxied to their gate, she turned to him and reached for his hand. "Rafe, I don't know what's real or not. You're right, there is something. But for now, it has to be on the back burner until I get my brother back."

Relief danced along his nerve endings. It was enough for now. "I'm fine with that. Just don't shut me out. We will make more headway working together."

"I promise. I…"

"I know. Who would have thought that a night in Norfolk could change so much?"

CHAPTER 6

The state department had called, just as Rafe predicted. When she'd gotten off the plane and checked her phone, she found a message from Lizzie. They now had a point of contact, a Mr. Ted Clement, who had called while she was on the plane. She'd let Rafe know too before they said goodbye and he went to catch his plane to Denver.

Neither of them wanted to say goodbye or turn away first. It was hard for Meghan to believe that she could feel this way about someone she'd just met. Rafe was like her Barbie Dream Date when she played that game with Lizzie when they were young. The man you fantasized about but knew there wasn't a chance in hell he even existed. Yet, there he was, and he was claiming her as his own.

She'd tried to deny it, but when he'd taken her in his arms and kissed her in the airport her knees gave out. It really was like out of some romance novel. But it was real. Heart racing, cheeks flushed, and damp panties didn't lie. If it wasn't love, she was heavy in lust. Too bad it was happening at the worst time of her life.

Reluctantly she stepped away from him, and he just as reluctantly let her go. He promised to text her as soon as he landed in Denver and if he heard anything else from his mysterious friend, Tex. As she watched him walk away from her to his gate, she blinked back tears that threatened to overflow. Her emotions were raw, but she needed to pull it together since she had no idea what she'd be walking into at her sister's house.

If she'd forgotten it was Saturday, she remembered as soon as she opened the door and was assailed by the aroma of pancakes. Pancake Day was a tradition in the Butler household and nothing and no one stood in the way of Lizzie's famous blueberry pancakes.

As much as she wanted to talk to her sister about Charlie, the state department and Rafe she had to wait. The scent of pancakes triggered more stomach growling and she smiled as she thought about Rafe's response when it growled last. Hard to believe it was only about ten hours ago. It felt more like last year.

"I'm here," Meghan yelled as she closed the front door. Two children and a fifty-pound dog came barreling around the corner and threw themselves at her. Thankfully, she was close enough to the front door that she didn't end up at the bottom of a pile of bodies and fur.

"Hey, give Aunt Meghan a break. She's been up all night," Lizzie yelled from the kitchen.

"Sorry, Aunt Meghan," her niece Lia said as she gave her a hug.

"Me too, kinda," CJ, also known as Craig Junior, chimed in before hugging her tight enough to cut off her circulation.

"I guess you're sorry too, Stanley?" Meghan asked the fluffy mutt and was given a woof and the thumping of his tail hitting the wood floor.

"Meghan?" Kathy Henley said as she came into the living room in her slippers and bathrobe. Her mom looked tired.

"Hi, Mom. Did you enjoy the slumber party last night?" Meghan replied as she walked over and gave her mom a hug and a kiss and was surprised how frail she seemed. She'd need to check with the aides and see if Lizzie had any updates from the doctor. One more thing to add to her to do list while she was visiting.

"C'mon into the kitchen. I can't leave these pancakes they'll burn."

"Oh no. It would be a travesty. We can't have the best pancakes in the southern hemisphere burn."

"Meghan, you're just being silly now. The pancakes aren't that good," her mom said.

"They are too. Right, kids?"

"Yes. Yes. Yes," they yelled as they ran past her into the kitchen.

Lizzie was standing in front of the stove, a spatula in one hand and a pitcher of pancake batter in the other. It was a sight to behold, and one of the best things about coming to visit.

"How long until it's ready?" Meghan asked as she looked at the plate piled high with pancakes and the bowl filled with bacon.

"One more batch. But if the kids would set the table, y'all can get started."

"No, we won't," Kathy said. "We'll all sit together and eat like a civilized family. You know the rules.

Lizzie turned and winked at her. It'd had been the house rules when they were living at home. Everyone ate together and no one got up from the table until everyone was finished. Lizzie didn't keep that rule at her house except when Mom was visiting. As hungry as Meghan was, she'd live. It was good to be home.

The food disappeared almost as soon as it was placed on the table. Anyone watching would think they'd been starved for weeks. Pancakes had an extremely limited lifespan in the Butler house. There wasn't a person who tried them that didn't crave them afterward.

Lizzie shared the recipe with Meghan, but she'd never made them. It was part of the visit she looked forward to whenever she could make it back home. It was also the only time she ate so many carbs in a day. Her hips were groaning just knowing the number of calories she'd ingested from the pancakes, syrup, and bacon. Thank God for the fat-free half and half.

The other bad part about carbs was the after effects. All she wanted to do was close her eyes for a little bit. It might have also been that she'd been up all night. It didn't matter, she needed to know what her sister found out from the state department guy and wanted to check to see if Rafe arrived in Denver. She hadn't been able to check her phone while at the table either, another rule, but this one was Lizzie's and there were no exceptions ever for anyone.

They all helped to clear the dishes and make sure the kitchen was clean. Then the kids were allowed to escape to their rooms so the grown-ups could talk. Exhausted and with her patience on a short leash, Meghan forced herself to take a few deep breaths. It reminded her of Rafe getting her through the panic attack and she smiled. But it worked, she had her emotions reigned in again.

"What's got you smiling?" Lizzie asked as she sat down on the sofa next to her. She could have kissed her when she saw the two steaming mugs she'd placed on the table.

"Oh my God. Thank you."

"I figured you could use some more. Did you get any sleep last night?"

"Nope. Not a wink. Did you?"

"Not much. And nothing after Mr. Clement called."

"Where's Mom?"

"She went to lie down. She's been sleeping a lot more. I figured the pancakes probably didn't hurt either. Perfect for a slow Saturday morning."

"Is that why you started the tradition?"

"Yup. There's a method to my madness. It even keeps the kids down to a dull roar so Craig and I can just sit back and relax for a little while. When he's here," Lizzie said and sighed. "That's not much anymore. He's been traveling so much."

"I'm sorry…"

"Don't be. When he gets the promotion, it will all be worth it."

"I'm sure." Meghan was trying to figure out how to get her back on track. She needed all the information possible about Charlie. And she still hadn't heard from Rafe.

"Not to be a pain, because I really do care, but did Clement say anything other than what you sent in the text?" As she finished her sentence her phone buzzed, and she pulled it out of her pocket. Thank goodness.

Hey Spitfire. I'm finally in Denver. Rocky trip. No news from Tex yet. I'll call you if I hear anything. Xoxo

"Spitfire? Are you holding out on me?"

"Huh?" She'd been re-reading his text hearing every word in his voice, and she hadn't realized her sister was looking at her screen.

"Who is in Denver and who is Tex?"

It's not like she planned on keeping Rafe a secret from Lizzie or anyone, but there hadn't been a chance to talk about anything with the kids and their mother around.

"It's a bit of a long story. And I'll tell you after I know for sure you told me everything you know about Charlie."

"Of course, I did. Why would I hold back?"

"I'm not saying you are. But it's crazy that we don't know anything other than that they were taken hostage. You'd think we've have heard something else by now."

"It just happened though. Maybe they need time to find out more?"

"I'm sure they do. But we don't really know when it happened, only when the news broke the story. It could have happened a few days ago."

"Shit. I didn't think about that." Lizzie's eyes welled up with tears. It's not the reaction Meghan was trying to get. Lizzie was the softy of the family, followed by Charlie. It had always been on Meghan to keep them strong. She'd been the most like their mom. Kathy Henley's nickname had been the Rock of Gibraltar because when she made up her mind nothing and no one could persuade her otherwise. It was also because when the shit hit the fan, Kathy was always there, the tower of strength in any crisis. It all changed after their father had a heart attack and died three years ago, and then her

Alzheimer's diagnosis. Now it was up to Meghan to be the rock of the family.

"I'm sorry. I've had too much time thinking about this. The lack of information is killing me."

"I know. I feel like we should be doing something."

"Exactly. But he's in Afghanistan. Or he was. They could have taken them out of the country to hide them." After catching the look of horror on Lizzie's face, she realized she needed to keep most of her thoughts to herself. They weren't going to do anything except get her sister riled up.

"Ugh. Don't listen to me. I'm a writer remember, over-active imagination." Meghan pulled her sister into a hug.

"You're right. And I need to stay in control for the kids."

"And mom. Maybe more for mom. I'm not sure what this would do to her."

Lizzie nodded and grabbed a mug of coffee and took a big sip. Then she turned back to Meghan.

"Okay, you've stalled long enough. Fess up. I want to know everything about that text message. Don't hold back because I'll know if you try." Dammit. She would too.

In an attempt to put off the inquisition for a tad bit longer, Meghan grabbed the other mug of coffee. There were so many emotions twisting inside she wasn't sure what to say. Forefront was worry about Charlie, then there was Rafe. Oh boy. Her sister was going to enjoy this conversation.

"The text is from a guy named Rafe. He was one of the other stranded passengers."

"Okay…" Lizzie was eating this up with a spoon.

"Since we were stuck for so long and most of the airport was closed, we had dinner together. He's nice."

"Nice? Bullshit. You never say 'nice'."

"Fine. He's drop-dead gorgeous. Are you happy now?"

"Sort of. How did you go from dinner with drop-dead gorgeous to him texting you? And who the heck is Tex?"

"It was a long night."

"I'll bet," Lizzie said with a smirk. She was going to have to take a bunch of crap, but it would be worth it to see Lizzie smile. It also made Rafe's actions of the night before more understandable. She owed him an apology for her freak out.

"He was sitting near me at the gate when they announced the delay. I may have grumbled something about the plane loud enough for him to hear me."

"Uh huh…"

"He had a point and we chatted a bit, then stood on line to update our tickets, and he asked me if I'd like to have dinner with him."

"And you said yes? To a stranger?"

"We were in the airport. What could have happened?"

"Hey, I watch those shows on the Discovery Channel. He could have pulled you out of sight and raped you or murdered you or worse."

"What's worse than rape or murder?" Meghan laughed, because really. That was pretty much the top echelon of horrible.

"Whatever."

"I may have forgotten to tell you he was in the Navy." The look on Lizzie's face said she wasn't buying his being in the service as a good enough reason. "I don't know how to explain it. There's just something about him."

Reaching for the other mug, Lizzie took a drink, and then sat with her legs crossed Indian style. She was definitely invested in the story now.

"Don't stop now."

"I guess it was the way he helped me when I found out about Charlie. We were at a bar. It was the only place still open. A Special Report came on the TV and I knew it was his group. I just knew it." Her voice got thick with tears, but she wasn't going to let them fall. Not now. When Charlie came back to them, then she'd cry.

"Probably the same thing I saw. I threw up in the bathroom. Thank God the kids were in bed already."

Meghan agreed. They'd managed to keep the news about Uncle Charlie from the ten-year-old twins so far, but there was no telling how long they'd be able to keep it quiet.

"He got me back to our table and bought me a drink. It helped take some of the chill away."

Lizzie nodded. "So, he's good in a crisis?"

"Hell yeah. I didn't find out until a few hours later but he's not just in the Navy. He's a SEAL. So yeah, I'd say he's amazing in a crisis. He's also funny, smart, and when I look into his chocolate brown eyes I could stay there forever."

"Damn. You've got it bad. Love in an Airport. Sounds like one of my romance novels."

"Funny you say that. It's what I said to him."

"He feels the same way?"

"That's what he says."

"Maybe something good will come out of all of this. You've been alone way too long. It would be great if you found your someone."

Meghan had to agree. Not that she'd been looking but it looked like the universe had other ideas. "Did you ask him to help us find Charlie? He must have connections, right?"

"I did. He can't help and he explained why. But what he didn't initially tell me is he has a friend— Tex—that is some kind of computer genius. Rafe asked him to see what he could find out."

"That's great. He won't get into trouble, will he?"

"I don't think so. I guess he does this kind of

stuff a lot. But he was able to confirm that it was Charlie's group that was taken."

"So, you knew before you got my text?"

"Yeah but only by about an hour."

"I guess hearing it from two separate people means there's no doubt." Lizzie's voice lost the earlier animation that had been there when they were talking about Rafe. Reality sucked, but also couldn't be avoided.

"Did he find out anything else?"

"No, not yet. If he has, he hasn't let Rafe know yet. That's what he said."

"And where is he now?"

"Rafe? Denver. He was on leave going to visit his sister and her kids."

"Wow, I'd say you've got quite a story for the grandkids. I met your grandpa in an airport when I was stranded. And he helped us save your Great Uncle Charlie…"

"Who saved Uncle Charlie?" Kids. Guaranteed to hear you when you didn't want them to but not hear a thing when you wanted something.

"No one."

"Sam said that there were missionaries kidnapped in Ganistan. Is that where Uncle Charlie is?"

"When did you talk to Sam?"

"We're playing our game and he messaged me."

"You let him play online? He's only ten,"

Meghan almost growled at her sister. What was she thinking?

"I monitor them, and it's only the one game. Basketball. No killing or anything." Meghan rolled her eyes. Her sister was beyond naïve sometimes. "Uncle Charlie is fine. You only have twenty more minutes before you need to shut down the game."

"Can we please have a little longer?"

"No. What did I say?"

"But it's Saturday. I don't have any homework left."

"No. Aunt Meghan is here and Grannie. We're going to do something together." That elicited not only another eye roll from Meghan but one from CJ. She'd been hoping to take a nap after they'd finished their chat. Looks like that was going to be out of the question.

CHAPTER 7

The flight from Atlanta to Denver had seen non-stop turbulence. Rocky was an extreme understatement. It was nice to be back on solid ground. Following the throng of people, he made his way to the rental car area to get his car. Except they didn't have one. Perfect.

This trip had been FUBAR from the moment he'd stepped into Norfolk Airport—except for Meghan. So maybe he had to deal with all this shit to have found his woman. He'd been through worse, he'd deal. It would be a lot easier after he had a hot shower and a couple of hours of shut-eye.

"We're sorry. If you could give us about ten minutes, we should have one for you."

"Okay. Thanks." It wouldn't pay to give the counter guy a hard time, it wasn't his fault. He was supposed to pick up the car yesterday, it's not surprising that they rented it to someone else. In the scheme of things, what was another ten minutes? It gave him a chance to give Tex a call.

"Rafe. Bet you're glad to be on the ground?"

"How. Never mind. And fuck yes. It was rough."

"It looked like it."

"Did you find out anything else? Anything I can tell Meghan?"

"Some but not enough. My regular channels were down. I had to go deeper."

"I'm guessing that's not normal?"

"No. Not for something like this. It's not military or classified, it should have been easy."

"Sounds like someone is hiding something."

"You're right. Except it's a someone, not a something. The Georgia senator's daughter to be exact."

"What? She's part of that group?"

"Yup. And they don't want anyone to know it. Understandable, if the Taliban finds out they have an HVT it will go one of two ways and both will end in a bloodbath."

Rafe whistled just under his breath. No shit. Talk about a high-value target. "Fuck me running."

"In a word or three. I'm surprised you haven't been spun up yet."

"I'm sure it's coming, it's our section."

"What are you going to tell Meghan?"

"I don't know. Once the team is read in, I can't tell her anything. This sucks donkey balls."

"Glad I'm not in your shoes. I did some digging

into her too. She's smart, cares about others, takes care of her family. She's got the brother and a sister. The sister is married with twins. Her dad passed away three years ago after a heart attack. Her mother is still alive but was diagnosed with Alzheimer's six months ago."

"Holy shit. I didn't ask you to do that."

"I know. But I wanted to make sure you weren't getting yourself into anything that could fuck you later."

"Thanks, I think. Anything else? Want to tell me when she lost her virginity?"

"I could… "

"I was kidding."

"So was I."

"Mr. Rafe Buchanan, please come to the Enterprise Service Desk."

"Gotta go, my car is ready."

"I'll keep looking. If I find anything I'll get in touch."

"Thank you, Tex. I appreciate you doing this more than I can say."

"No problem. I'm happy to help."

THE DRIVE to his sister's passed without incident. It was nice that at least one part of the trip had. The kids were excited as always to see him and jumped on him as soon as he walked in the door. He'd been prepared, it was their usual greeting. His sister, Dawn, was another story. The dark circles under her eyes would have been enough, but her complexion was sallow. Had she been sick again?

He begged her every time to let him help her. But she was as stubborn as he was and repeatedly refused, claiming her job and the benefits she got from the government were enough. Bob was active duty when he was killed, and even though she got monthly payments for her and the kids it was hard for her to make ends meet. If she'd move to Virginia, he could help and take the kids for the weekend, but she didn't want to take them away from their home. He understood, but they were his only family and he wanted to do more for them.

"Uncle Rafe, wait till you see how good I'm getting at basketball."

"Great. I can't wait."

"Can you come now?"

"I want to say hi to your mom and your sister, is that okay?"

"I guess so," Chase said, and it was obvious he wasn't happy. Rafe hid his smile. They were always so excited to see him, and he couldn't blame them for wanting to monopolize his time. Hell, he loved being with them.

Cindy, Chase's sister, held on to his hand like she was afraid he'd disappear. "Hi, sweetheart. How are you? Do you have something you want to show me too?"

"Yeah. But I can wait." Quiet, reserved, just like her mom. He worried she'd hide in the background behind Chase and get lost.

"Kids, give Uncle Rafe a chance to get inside the door at least. Geesh. He's been stuck in an airport all night. He probably needs a nap."

"Naps are for babies, Mom. Uncle Rafe is a SEAL. He doesn't need naps." And there you have it, out of the mouths of children.

Dawn shrugged her shoulders and smiled. "No nap for you. Sorry."

"It's okay. I kind of figured that would happen. Can you make a pot of coffee and pour it in a pitcher for me?"

"You're kidding, right?"

"Maybe," he said with a wink as he took four steps to pull his sister into a big bear hug. "How are you doing, sis?"

"Fine, great."

"Liar."

"Hey, you can't fault a girl for trying. Seriously though, it's all good. I'm just a little tired. We all had the flu and it's taking a while to get back to normal."

"Why didn't you call me?"

"And what would you have done from halfway across the country? I'm a big girl, you don't have to protect me. You need to find your own woman to protect." If she only knew. It made him think about Meghan and how she was doing with her family.

73

Had she gotten any more information from the state department? He still needed to let her know he arrived.

"Wait. What's that look on your face? Rafe Buchanan, you found a woman."

"Where is she Uncle Rafe, I want to see her," Cindy asked. She reminded him of a little doll, and he picked her up to give her a hug.

"She didn't come with me this time. But I promise you'll get to meet her soon enough."

"Okay."

"Why don't you give Uncle Rafe and I a chance to talk for a few minutes."

"But Mommmmm…."

"Hey, buddy. Listen to your mom. Give me a chance to chill for a few minutes and then we'll go play some ball." Rafe waited for him to put up more of a fight.

"All right. But don't take too long."

"I won't."

"Me and my doll can watch, right Uncle Rafe?"

"Yes, you can." Chase rolled his eyes, and Rafe remembered exactly what it was like to have a little sister want to tag along. It's how Dawn had been and eventually, she'd fallen in love and married his best friend.

"Coffee or something stronger?" Dawn asked as she headed into the kitchen.

"I better stick with coffee." He'd followed her and sat at the table.

"Wouldn't you rather sit in the other room. The couch is a heck of a lot more comfortable than that chair."

"Nah, we're closer to the coffee pot here."

Dawn shook her head as she filled two mugs. Pushing one in front of him, she sat across the table. "What's going on? You seem distracted."

"I'm not…"

When she quirked an eyebrow, he was busted. As soon as she became a mom there was no putting anything over on her. It's like giving birth gave a woman some kind of secret powers.

"Fine. The woman I met, her name is Meghan, her brother was kidnapped by the Taliban."

"Shiiioooot. What are you doing here then? Why aren't you with her?"

He winced, this part might not go well. "I met her at the airport while we were stranded in Norfolk." He gave her a minute to digest what he'd said but she didn't say a word. Just waited for what he'd say next.

"There was something about her, I can't explain it. I convinced her to have dinner with me. It was going well and then she saw the news report."

"Oh my God. I can't even imagine what she's feeling right now. And no, I'm not shocked. You forget that the first time I hung out with you and Bob I came in and told Mom he was going to be my husband."

"Shit, you're right. I'd forgotten. Do you think it runs in the family?"

"Who knows, but as long as you're happy I'm happy. What's she like?"

"She's a spitfire. Kind, funny, but hard as nails, all packed into a little body that can't be five foot tall."

Laughing, Dawn almost choked on her coffee. "Sounds like your perfect match."

"Yeah, she does, doesn't she? I had a hard time convincing her it was meant to be. Did I say she was smart and stubborn?"

"I think I'm going to like her."

"Oh yeah, you will."

"Does she live in Norfolk near you?"

"No, she lives and works in DC. She was in town visiting a friend. But she was going to Atlanta from there to visit her family."

"I still think you should have gone with her."

"To be honest, I was tempted. But I've been looking forward to seeing you and the kids. I hate that I had to postpone it so many times. I just hope we get through the week without me having to leave early."

"That sounds like you already know something is going to happen."

Rafe shrugged. There was nothing he could tell her. Besides he only had the intel that Tex had shared, it hadn't come from command yet. Maybe it would all be resolved without needing them.

"You know the drill. I can get called in at any time. But we're all on leave so hopefully, we'll be good."

"How are you? You look tired, and I swear there's a little grey in your hair now."

"Bull shit."

"Hey, the kids. I don't need Chase saying that at school. I get enough phone calls from his teacher already."

"Has he been getting into trouble? What's been going on? You should have called me."

"What are you going to do from two thousand miles away?"

"I could talk to him on the phone, or we could Skype."

"He's ten, he misses his father. I've been taking him to counseling. I think it's helping. And before you say it, no we're not moving to Virginia. This is our home."

"But if I were closer, you said it yourself..."

"No, I said you're not here. We're fine. Their friends are here, my job is here. This is just something we have to learn how to live with."

Dawn was tough. She and Bob had twelve years together before he'd been killed in action. It had been hard for him when they'd started dating. Bob was his best friend, and then he wanted to spend time with his sister. Teenage boys could be real jerks.

"I'm not trying to run your life. I worry about

you and the kids. Now that Mom and Dad are gone, you're here alone."

"I've never wanted to live anywhere else. This is home, Rafe. I'm not like you. I never wanted to travel or see the world. I was always happy here. I hated when we had to move around when Bob was given new orders."

"Okay. But promise me if you need help with anything, you'll call me. I know I make you promise every time, but I hope eventually you'll actually call me."

Dawn laughed. He knew her as well as she knew him. They'd gotten closer as they got older and they were the only family they had left.

"Uncle Rafe, is it time yet?"

"Honestly, I'm surprised they left us alone this long."

"It's okay. We can talk more after they go to bed."

"Do we have to?" Dawn said doing her best whiny child impersonation. She did it well. He figured she had a lot of practice from hearing it.

"Let me change clothes and I'll be right with you, Chase."

"Yay."

"You have no idea what you're getting yourself into," Dawn said while shaking her head. "He's going to run you ragged."

"I'm a Navy SEAL. You can't possibly think a ten-year-old boy can wear me out?"

"We'll see. When was the last time you slept?"

"I don't remember, a couple of days probably. Don't worry about me. I'm good." He picked up his bag that he'd left in the living room and as he climbed the stairs, he could still hear Dawn laughing.

After a quick trip to the bathroom to brush his teeth and wash up, he checked his phone for messages. Nothing from Tex yet. He wasn't sure if that was good news or not. He wanted to call Meghan and hear her voice, but then he wouldn't want to hang up and he had Chase waiting on him, so a text would have to do.

Hi Spitfire. How's it going? I'm at my sister's. No new info. Sorry.

As he rummaged in his bag for his jeans and sneakers, his phone pinged.

I'm glad you got there ok. I bet they were happy to see you. It's ok here. No more news either. I hate waiting.

I'll give Tex a call in a bit but if he had anything, he'd let me know. SD didn't call again?

While he waited for her answer he finished getting changed.

SD = State Dept? Then no. Nothing. Asshats. They have to know more than they're saying.

Unfortunately, he knew they did, so did he, but he couldn't tell her either. If the Senator's daughter was part of Charlie's missionary group, then it would be a huge media nightmare if it got out.

I'll check in later. I have a date with a kid and a basketball.

Have fun!

Love you. Xoxo

Rafe was halfway down the stairs before his phone pinged again. When he saw her message, nothing could have wiped the smile off his face.

Love you too.

CHAPTER 8

"Is that him?"

"Yeah," Meghan answered.

"Sweet Jesus you have it bad."

"Why do you say that?"

"You should see the look on your face," Lizzie said with a smile. "It's about time you have someone in your life that can make you look like that. I'd about given up hope."

"Gee thanks. It's not like I'm eighty."

"No, but you never do anything to try to find someone either."

"Apparently, I didn't need to go out and look. He just sort of fell into my lap." They both laughed at that. Too bad it had to happen on one of the worst days of her life.

"I'm so freakin' tired, but I don't think I can sleep. Did the state department guy leave a phone number?"

"Yeah, let me get it."

"What are you girls whispering about?"

"Nothing, Mom."

Lizzie walked back into the room with the piece of paper. "Meggy has a boyfriend."

"You do? It's about time. I thought you were going to be an old maid."

Meghan rolled her eyes. Her mother was going to go on about this unless something distracted her, bless her heart. The Alzheimer's made her forgetful and she would talk about the same thing over and over again.

"I asked you not to call me that. I don't need your kids picking it up."

"Why not? It's cute."

"When I was ten maybe, not now."

"Don't be silly, Meggy fits you, dear. Your father loved the name. You know you're named after his mom. He doted on you…"

It could have been worse, of all the repeat stories, Meghan loved the ones about her father.

But now that mom was there, they couldn't call the guy from the state department. They needed to keep the information about Charlie from her for as long as they could. Neither of them knew how she'd react to it, or if she understood most of what they were saying at times. Every week she'd gotten a little worse. Soon she'd need someone to be with her around the clock.

"I think I'm going to go upstairs and try to get a little sleep."

"But you just...," Lizzie stopped herself mid-sentence and nodded. "I have your room made up."

"Great, thank you. See you in a little while."

"You just got here, Meg, you can't leave yet."

"I'm not leaving, Mom. Just going upstairs to take a little nap. I'll see you in a bit."

"Oh okay, dear. Give me a kiss."

Meghan dropped a kiss on her mom's cheek. It always amazed her how soft her skin was, like silk. No matter how much she aged that was the one thing that hadn't changed.

After she got into her room, she unpacked her bag, took off her makeup, and pulled her laptop out of its case. As she waited for it to boot up, she grabbed her phone and re-read Rafe's last message. Lizzie was right, she did have it bad. But it was a good thing she'd checked because the battery was almost dead.

"Now where did I put that cord?" Rummaging through her bag, she finally came up with it. After getting it plugged in and making sure the volume was on, she put it on the nightstand and settled back against the pillows and grabbed the laptop.

The first thing she did was send an email to Charlie's missionary group hoping someone would have more information. Ten of their people were missing, they had to know more than the news reported.

Even though Rafe's friend hadn't found anything else, it didn't mean that there hadn't been more in the news. She hadn't seen anything since the initial report in Norfolk. It was very strange, as she searched site after site there was nothing other than what she already knew. There was no follow up news at all. They didn't even mention where the group was based.

An American missionary group was kidnapped and there was a news blackout. Something was very wrong. As a last ditch effort to dig up anything at all, she called her job. It was a major newspaper, surely someone had picked up the story and investigated. And she knew just who to call. Checking to make sure there was enough charge on the phone, she took a deep breath and dialed his number.

"Josephs."

"Hey Marty, it's Meghan Henley."

"Who?" Seriously? Could he be a bigger asshat?

"Meghan Henley. Society page. Three desks over from yours?"

"Ahh right. What's up? I don't have time for small talk I'm in the middle of filing my story."

"This won't take long. Do you have any news about the Missionary Group that was kidnapped in Afghanistan yesterday?"

"Huh." She could hear his fingers on his keyboard. He hadn't heard a word she'd said.

"Marty."

"What?"

"Did you hear me?"

"I heard something like blah blah blah."

"Why are you such an ass?" He actually chuckled. It figured that he heard that.

"Because I'm the best and can do what I want."

"Of course, you are. Can you be human for a minute? Please? I need to know if you heard anything about the kidnapped missionary group."

It was quiet on the other end of the phone. He'd actually stopped typing. Unless he'd hung up on her, that was entirely possible. She was about to disconnect and call him back when he answered.

"I saw something yesterday but that's it."

"Don't you think that's weird?"

"Maybe. I don't know. It could have been a false report."

"It wasn't."

"How can you be sure? We get shit like that all the time."

"That's crap. We don't get reports of false kidnappings in the middle east."

"Listen, Miss Society Page, how would you know?"

"Because I follow the news, I don't want to be the society page forever."

"Why are you bugging me about this?"

"Because my brother is in that missionary group." For a moment there was silence.

"Fuck. Are you sure?"

"Yes. Totally."

"No, I meant are you sure they've been kidnapped. If they were really missing it would be all over the news. AP would have filed a follow-up story."

It was exactly what Meghan had been thinking. It should have been. So why wasn't it?

"I've got to get this filed." Before she could answer he'd hung up. Asshat. But she got the information or more like non-information that she needed.

Not sure what to do next, she stared at the laptop screen with the one and only story about the kidnapping. As she read through it for the tenth time there was a knock on her door.

"Meghan? Are you awake?"

"Yeah, come on in."

Lizzie opened the door while she balanced a tray with cookies and milk. She was turning into their mom, but it was kind of nice.

"Cookies?"

"Thanks," Meghan answered as she grabbed a warm chocolate chip cookie and took a bite.

"Did you find out anything yet? Did you talk to the guy from the state department?"

"No and no."

"Nothing?"

"Not really. I've searched every place I can find on the internet and there is nothing other than the original story from yesterday. Then I called the paper. They haven't gotten anything either."

"How is that possible? There are ten people missing," Lizzie said, her voice wobbly from holding back tears.

"I know, Lizzie." Meghan reached out and squeezed her sister's hand. "Let's call that guy now. Maybe he can tell us what's going on."

"Okay."

Dialing the number from the paper Lizzie had given her downstairs, she listened to the phone ring. After the fifth ring, it went to voicemail.

"You've reached the desk of Ted Clement. I can't take your call right now. If you leave your name and number and what this is in reference to, I'll get back to you as soon as possible." Son of a bitch.

"This is Meghan Henley. You spoke to my sister yesterday. Our brother is part of the missionary group that was kidnapped. Please call us back. We need to know what's going on, and what you're doing to get him back."

"He didn't answer?"

"Nope, it went straight to voicemail."

"Ugh. Why give us a number if we can't reach him?"

"It's the weekend. Maybe he only works Monday through Friday?"

"But he's in the government. Aren't they supposed to handle this stuff no matter when it happens?"

"Lizzie, it'll be okay. I promise. I don't know what normal procedure is."

87

"You can't promise. We don't even know if Charlie is still alive." There was no holding back her tears. She pulled Lizzie into a hug and let her cry. It was like the dam had been opened and the flood waters poured out. She'd held it all in since last night and she needed the release.

All cried out, Lizzie pulled out of her arms and went to the bathroom to grab a tissue. Meghan wanted to throw something she was so frustrated. Why couldn't she find out anything? They were family, they had a right to know.

Lizzie came back carrying a box of tissues and sat on the bed. "So now what do we do?"

"I'm not sure. I wrote to the general email at the Deliver Hope Ministry. I checked to see if they wrote back while you were in the bathroom. Nothing so far."

"Unbelievable. I feel like I'm in the Twilight Zone. How can no one know anything?"

"I feel the same way. There has to be more to this and that's why they are keeping it quiet. Do you know the other people in his group?"

"Umm. Yes. Actually, he left me a list with all of their names, where they were going to be and when. I think I have it in my room. Be right back."

Meghan wanted to go with her to search but she stayed put. It would only make Lizzie crazy if she started tearing the place apart. She'd just have to cool her jets and wait.

"I've got it." Thank God. Meghan was about to

lose her mind by the time Lizzie returned and handed her the typed sheet of paper. They'd all learned to be organized from their father. He'd had a mild case of OCD and nothing could ever be out of place.

As she perused the list nothing seemed out of the ordinary until she got to the second to last name. There was something familiar about it. Typing the name into search it took all of one second to give her the answer.

"Sweet baby Jesus."

"What?" Lizzie pushed over to sit next to her and look at her screen. "Is that Senator Stanhope's daughter?"

"Yes. I thought the name sounded familiar."

"Why isn't it all over the news then? Her father is a senator."

"Exactly. If they realize they have a senator's daughter and not just a bunch of preachers, it will be much worse."

"I didn't think of that."

"I wouldn't if it wasn't for the job. I look for different angles, think about things differently. And I'd bet a million dollars it's why there's nothing out there right now."

"I want Charlie back. There's got to be something we can do."

"We will, Lizzie. We'll figure out something. Hopefully, Rafe's friend can help."

"How can he help?"

"Supposedly he's some kind of computer genius who can find out anything about anything."

"He's a spy?"

"I don't think so. Rafe said he was a SEAL but lost his leg and was medically retired."

"He could still be a spy."

"Maybe, but I don't think Rafe would have told me about him then."

"That's true. Can you call him? Maybe he found out something else."

"Rafe or the computer guy?" Meghan wasn't sure Rafe would want her passing Tex's name around so for now, he'd just be the computer guy.

"The computer guy."

"No, I don't have his contact information. Rafe promised he'd call later. He's playing basketball with his nephew."

"How old is his nephew?"

"Same age as the twins, ten. He's also got a niece who is eight. Awful nosy, aren't you?"

"If he's interested in my sister then I think I have a right to know. Looks like lots of kids at the family reunions."

"Don't you think you're jumping the gun a little? I just met the guy."

"Sweet girl, you're living in fantasy land if you don't see it. Your face lit right up when you read his text messages. I think I'm right on target."

Meghan didn't know how to answer that. It's not like she could disagree with Lizzie, but she wasn't ready to own up to it either. Charlie needed their focus. If a relationship with Rafe was meant to be then it would happen.

"We'll see. Right now, my focus is on getting Charlie and his group back."

"Agreed. But it is nice to see you thinking about something other than work, and I don't mean Charlie." After she finished talking, Lizzie stuck her tongue out. It was like they were five and seven again. Next, she'd say she was going to tell mom on her. Well maybe not. She had to deal with her own children now.

"Fine. Now, why don't you check on the kids and I'm going to try to get some sleep since we just have to wait."

"I'll come and get you for dinner."

"I'll be down before that."

Lizzie nodded as she walked out of the bedroom and pulled the door shut. Meghan put the laptop aside after checking for emails one more time. Waiting sucked donkey balls. With a yawn, she leaned back against the pillows and closed her eyes.

CHAPTER 9

Rafe wouldn't admit it to Dawn, but it hadn't been easy keeping up with Chase. The kid was a bundle of energy and after being up all night his energy stores were lower than usual. Or his age might be catching up to him, but he'd fight it off for as long as possible.

The whole Black Eagle Team was getting older. It was hard to believe that they were one of the oldest active teams. Most of them had been together since BUD/S. Jake Warner, their Master Sergeant, had picked them and managed to keep them alive through it all. When he'd added Cam Patterson a few years ago, Rafe hadn't been sure he'd fit in. The kid was young and hot-headed but after a few months he'd settled in and become part of the team. Halo, his K-9, didn't have his handler's problem, he'd fit in right away. They loved that dog, and he'd saved their asses more than once.

After the game, he'd checked his phone for messages. There was still nothing from Tex or anyone else. He was getting antsy and imagined his little spitfire was probably bouncing off the walls. If he'd been in her shoes, he'd have been on a plane to Afghanistan as soon as he'd gotten the news even if it meant going AWOL. It was family and he worried she'd try to do something like it.

The bed called to him after he got out of the shower. It was tempting. Too tempting. But he needed answers and Meghan did too. He'd made her a promise and he intended to keep it.

As he pulled his t-shirt over his head the phone rang. Grabbing it, he answered without looking at the caller. "Hey, Tex. About time, bro. I was just about to call you."

"Not Tex, but I sure as hell would like to know what information you're waiting for from him."

"Boss," Shit he was in trouble now. Jake knew Tex, they all did, but he also knew he wouldn't just call him to shoot some shit.

"It's complicated."

"Uncomplicate it, fast." Fuck. This wasn't going to go well.

"I was stuck overnight at the airport and I met a woman."

"Why didn't you just go home?"

"I could have, but I didn't want to leave her alone."

"Are you trying to compete with Murph now? Picking up women wherever you go?"

"Not even close. There was something about her. I can't explain it." No comment. Silence. Jake was already running scenarios in his head.

"Have you heard about the missionary group that was kidnapped?"

"As a matter of fact, yes."

"Her brother is one of the hostages."

"Fuck. That complicates things."

"You could say that."

"More than you realize. I'm sorry to fuck with your leave, but you need to get back to base asap."

"I'll get on the next available flight..."

"Just get to Buckley Air Force Base. There's a transport on stand-by. And tell Tex to stand down. Understand?"

"Copy that."

"See you soon, Rafe. Tell Dawn I'm sorry."

"I will." The whole team was on leave, and he wondered why they hadn't called in a different team. Jake hadn't briefed him on the mission, but he didn't need to be a mind reader to know where they were going. As much as he hated to leave, he wasn't disappointed. Not being able to tell Meghan anything wasn't going to go over well. His sister would understand, she'd been through it before. He hated having to leave so soon after he'd gotten there but it wasn't the first time.

He'd finished re-packing his bag when his

phone vibrated. This time he checked, half expecting it to be Meghan.

"Tex. Too bad you didn't call about fifteen minutes ago."

"Called in, huh?"

"You know it. Jake told me to tell you to stand down."

"How did he find out you called me?"

"Because I'm an ass and didn't check before I answered."

Tex snorted. "Do you want me to stand down?"

"Did you find out anything else?"

"Some. They haven't realized they have the senator's daughter. That's a good thing. But they haven't made demands yet either."

"Shit. Why take them then?"

"Not sure. But you'll probably know as much as I do soon."

"Maybe. You get better intel usually. Jake didn't say much at all. I was wondering if I could ask you a favor?"

"Sure. What's up?"

"Do you think you could keep Meghan in the loop for me? I can't tell her jack shit about anything and I'm worried she's going to get herself into trouble."

"She's yours, right?"

"Yeah. Even if she may not want to admit it yet."

"Then yeah, no problem. But you'd better let her

know who I am, so she doesn't freak out when I call her."

"Do you need her info?"

"Nah, I've got it already."

It was Rafe's turn to snort. Of course, he did. "I should have known. Thanks, bro. I appreciate it. This is going to get worse for her."

"Most likely. There's something weird with this whole thing. I'm not sure what it is yet, but I will find out."

"Thanks. I appreciate it. I'll check in when I can."

"Happy hunting."

As he slung his bag over his shoulder, there was a quiet knock on his door.

"Come in." Cindy opened the door and when she saw him the smile disappeared from her face.

"You just got here. Why are you going away?"

"I have to sweetheart, I'm so sorry."

"But we didn't get to have our tea party."

"Next time, I promise."

"You said that last time." It sucked, he hated that he kept disappointing these kids. But it was his job. He dropped his bag and swooped her into his arms. Her tiny hands wrapped around his neck and she laid her face against his.

"If I could stay I would. But I have to save some people from very bad men."

"Like Captain America?"

"Yes, kind of, yes. But I don't have a cool shield like he does."

"I guess it's okay then. Will you come back when you're done?"

"I will try very hard, but I can't promise. Okay?"

"Okay." She leaned back and kissed his cheek. "I love you, Uncle Rafe."

"I love you too, Cindy. Be good for your momma."

"I'm always good. It's Chase who is always getting into trouble." Placing her on the floor, he grabbed his bag and took her hand. As they headed down the stairs, the sound of his sister yelling at Chase punctuated his niece's comment.

"See Uncle Rafe. I told you." Rafe squeezed Cindy's hand.

"Yes, you did. Let's see if we can fix this. Sound good?"

"Yup." Her sweet innocence squeezed his heart. They needed their father. Bob was killed in action a year ago, and they'd gone through a lot. He'd planned on taking some of the pressure off of Dawn. That had gone out the window when Jake called, but he could play referee before he left.

"Hey. What's going on?" Dawn turned toward his voice and she saw his bag. He caught a glimpse of tears in her eyes before she turned again. What the hell was going on?

"Chase and I are working it out. It's fine."

"It didn't sound fine. Cindy and I could hear

you guys upstairs. Chase, you should never yell at your mother. She deserves your respect. What would your dad say if he heard you?"

Whatever Chase had been about to say died before it came out of his mouth. He may only be ten, but both of them had grown up a lot in the last year. "I'm sorry, Mom."

Dawn pulled him into her arms and looked over his head and mouthed the words, "thank you" to Rafe. "I'm sorry too, buddy. I shouldn't yell either. I don't want to have to argue with you every time I tell you no to something."

"I'll try to be better."

"That's all I ask. I love you."

"I love you too, Mom."

"You fixed them, Uncle Rafe."

"I think they did it on their own, sweetheart." She pulled her hand out of his and ran to her mother, who opened her arms to include her in the hug. As he watched the little family, happiness seeped into his soul.

"I hate to break this up, but I have to go."

"But you just got here, Uncle Rafe," Chase said. His little face still red from tears and anger.

"I know, but like I told Cindy, I have to go get the bad guys."

"Can't someone else go?"

"I'm afraid not. But I'll come back as soon as I can."

"Wow, that didn't take long. Is it what you were worried about? Dawn asked.

"Yeah."

"Be careful."

"Always. Now I want one of those group hugs before I go." He had to admit, all that love was powerful, and it stayed with him as he boarded the transport to head back to Norfolk an hour and a half later.

The plane was airborne before he figured out what to tell Meghan. The only thing that made it better was that he'd be able to keep his promise and bring Charlie back home to her family. Not being able to tell her he was going was one of the hardest things he'd had to do.

Deciding to call rather than text, he dialed her number.

"Hello?" Damn, he'd woken her.

"Spitfire, it's Rafe. I'm sorry I woke you."

"No. I shouldn't have been sleeping still. Lizzie was supposed to wake me up after an hour. What time is it?"

"Eighteen hundred."

"In English please?"

He chuckled. "Six p.m. your time."

"Dammit. I should have been up hours ago. Where are you? It sounds like you're on a plane. I thought you were in Denver."

"I was, but I got called back. We've got a mission."

"And you can't tell me anything, right?" It hadn't taken her long to wake up.

"Right. I'm sorry. But it's classified."

"How long will you be gone?"

"I don't know. I will call you when we get back. I'm not sure if I'll be able to, but I'll try to check on you."

"What about Charlie? Did your friend find out anything else? I've had dead ends here."

"He did, but it wasn't much. Tex said they hadn't asked for ransom yet."

"I don't understand how a group of Americans can get taken and no one is doing anything, and there's nothing on the news or anywhere else. Only that first report we saw."

"I know. But I'm sure there's a good reason. Listen, Tex is going to call you if he finds out anything else so you won't be in the dark. I texted his number to you. If you need anything give him a call. He will do what he can to help you."

"Why would he do that? He doesn't even know me?"

"Two reasons, one he's a great guy and can't resist helping anyone. And two, because you're mine. That makes you family."

"But we..."

"Don't say it. We've talked about this. You're not allowed to chicken out"

"Me? Chicken out. No way."

"There's my Spitfire. I have to go. But I'll call as soon as I can."

"Please be safe. I didn't think I'd have to deal with worrying about you so soon."

"I'll be fine. Behave yourself."

"What? I can't hear you."

"Bye, Spitfire. I love you."

"Bye." Meghan hadn't said the words, but he knew in his heart she felt the same as he did. She'd taken the news better than he'd expected too. Unless she wasn't awake enough to process what he'd said. It was a good thing she'd have Tex in case she needed anything.

It was another three hours before they landed at Naval Station Norfolk. As soon as he got off the plane, he headed to command. With no interruptions on the flight, he was able to grab some shut-eye. It wasn't much but it was better than nothing and he'd learned years ago to sleep when he could. Not sure when they'd be shipping out, he'd take what he could get. It might be a while before he got any more.

"Nice of you to join us," Ryan McLaughlin teased as he walked through the door. "We've been waiting hours for you."

"Don't they say the best is worth waiting for?" Rafe replied with a grin. His team was family, not by blood but something more.

"Bullshit," Drew Murphy replied.

"Where's Cam?" Rafe asked as he stored his pack.

"Outside with Halo."

Before Rafe could ask if they'd heard anything else, the door opened and Master Chief Jake Warner, their boss, walked in followed by Cam and Halo. From the look on Jake's face, they weren't going to like what was coming.

"Good timing, Rafe. Briefing starts in ten."

"I beat Cam, why pick on me?"

"Why are you always giving me grief?" Cam asked as he grabbed a chair and Halo laid down on the floor beside him.

"Because you're new. It's our job."

"I was new two years ago, what the fuck, man?"

Jake laughed. "You will always be the new guy. Might as well get used to it."

They were already seated at the table when Captain Randall and their CIA liaison, Bill Lynch walked in.

"By now, I'm sure you've heard about the missionaries kidnapped in Bamyan Province. What you don't know is that Senator Stanhope's daughter is part of that group."

Jake glanced at Rafe. He knew him well enough to know he needed to keep his mouth shut. Rafe tipped his chin and Jake nodded back.

"Have they made any demands?" Murph was their bomb guy. If something needed to get blown up, he was the man. Sometimes Rafe wondered if he enjoyed it a little too much.

"Not yet. We're not sure they realize who've they've got either. But their silence is worrying JSOC. Bill will continue the briefing with what we know."

After a few clicks on his laptop, the whiteboard displayed a photo of Miranda Stanhope. "This is the senator's daughter. There are also nine others in the group. But she's the reason we're going in. The senator has been with POTUS since state notified him. We squashed the TV coverage to try to keep her identity on lockdown. But we've picked up some chatter that the Taliban is trying to sell the group for weapons."

"To who?" Jake asked.

"The Iranians, ISIS, you name it. There isn't anyone who wouldn't want to get their hands on a group of Americans."

"So, what's the plan?" Ryan asked. He hated the Taliban and took every chance he got to kill as many of them as possible.

"We've got drones surveilling trying to find a location on our HVT but so far we haven't dug up anything concrete."

"Wait, so you're going to drop us with no intel and we're going on a scavenger hunt?"

"Jake, stand down. Bill's doing the best he can," Captain Knox interjected.

"We need more than 'we think they're somewhere in the mountains'. How the hell can we plan for that?"

"We're working our sources. By the time we get to Kandahar, we should have verification of their location."

"And if you don't? Then we just go in blind?"

"If that's what it takes, then yes," Knox replied.

There was nothing else to say after that. This was what they did, follow orders. Go where no one else could go and do the impossible, it's what made them SEALs.

Bill didn't look any happier than the rest of them. "We'll know before we touch down."

Rafe sure as hell hoped so.

"Take care of what you need to. We're departing in two hours." And with that, the briefing was over. Brief was definitely the word for it, like basically nothing Rafe hadn't already known from Tex. This was going to be a clusterfuck of epic proportions if they didn't get more intel."

CHAPTER 10

The phone call with Rafe worried Meghan more than she'd let on. He'd be in danger wherever he was going, and she had a fairly good idea it was Afghanistan. She also knew that the senator's daughter would be their priority. The news broadcasts enough stories about rescues to know how the government worked. They'd go in for Miranda Stanhope and try to get the others, but she'd be their priority.

Charlie was her priority. Leaving them behind for whatever reason would not be acceptable and the only way to guarantee it wouldn't happen would be to go there herself. Using her job as cover she could probably get close, but she still had to make it to Afghanistan. That was the big problem. It's not like just anyone could hop on a plane to the middle of a war zone. The clock was ticking. The longer they were captives the better chance they'd be hurt or worse. Let's hope Rafe's secret weapon would be able to help her.

As Rafe promised, he'd sent Tex's information in a text, and also warned her not to do anything stupid. It was probably a good thing he was out of touch because he'd kill her himself if he found out her plans. Let's hope Tex was a little more accommodating. Going in as a journalist, she hoped she'd be able to find out who took her brother and where they were. Didn't everyone want to tell their stories to the world? It was the only plan she could come up with. It had better work.

Before she asked for Tex's help, she needed to have her plan intact. Maybe someone had written her back from the ministry. They were her best bet to find out where Charlie had gone, and maybe they'd gotten more information.

Meghan could have jumped for joy when she opened her email and saw a message from Deliver Hope Ministries. Clicking on it, she skimmed the contents, then went back and re-read it. They'd gotten an update from the state department, but they hadn't learned much more than she already knew. Their last location was in the Bamyan Province, wherever the fuck that was.

Allan Collins was the name on the email, and he'd included his phone number. Checking the time, she realized it was too late to call but she would first thing in the morning.

Opening Word, she started a file with everything she knew, questions she still needed answers to, and plans that needed to be made. Meghan wasn't sure how long she'd been at it when there was a knock on the door.

"Meg?" Lizzie slowly opened the door, probably expecting her to be asleep still. Meghan should be annoyed, she hadn't wanted to sleep the day away, but she felt so much better.

"I'm awake. Rafe called a bit ago."

"When I checked on you earlier, you looked so peaceful. I didn't have the heart to wake you up."

"It's okay. I needed it even if I didn't want to sleep the day away."

"It wasn't all day. Are you hungry? There are plenty of leftovers from dinner." It's like the mere mention of food made Meghan's stomach growl. It had the worst timing.

Lizzie laughed. "I'll take that as a yes. Do you want to come downstairs and have it at the table?"

"Yeah. Let me just wash up and brush my teeth and I'll be right down. Are the kids still awake?"

"Hopefully not. They went to bed an hour ago, but you could look in on them if you want."

"It's okay. I'll see them in the morning."

Lizzie nodded and went back out the bedroom door. Meghan got up and washed. Then grabbed her laptop and phone and headed downstairs. Lizzie wasn't going to like her plan, not even a little bit.

By the time she'd gotten down to the kitchen,

Lizzie had a whole meal laid out for her. Beef stew, salad, fresh rolls. Her sister really was just like her mom. Or maybe she was trying so hard because they were losing her slowly to the disease.

"You were busy while I was slacking. This looks and smells great."

"Thanks. But I had the stew in the crock pot. The bread machine helped with the rolls and salad is nothing. Just leave room for dessert."

"What is it?"

"Nope. That's a surprise if you eat your dinner."

"What am I ten?"

"No, you only act like it sometimes." Meghan was about to let her have it when she saw the expression on Lizzie's face and burst out laughing. She'd fallen for it yet again.

"Oh my God, this is delicious. You need to give me the recipe."

"You cook?"

"Sometimes."

Grabbing one of the rolls from the basket, Lizzie buttered it and took a bite. "Are you lonely?"

That question took Meghan by surprise. Was she lonely? Maybe. But she didn't give herself a chance to think about it. She kept busy all the time and when she had down time she'd call or go visit Chrissy. And now she had Rafe in her life. Although if she managed to get to Afghanistan, she wasn't sure how he'd react.

"I don't think so. I'm usually busy. And I have you and Chrissy."

"And Rafe?"

"We'll see. It feels real but with all that's going on, who knows."

"You could come back here. Stay with us until you get a job. Or with Mom."

"I appreciate the offer, but I want my dream."

"We worry about you."

"You mean you worry about me. I am not sure what Mom does or doesn't remember."

Lizzie's eyes welled with tears and Meghan could have kicked herself. Maybe it was Lizzie who was lonely and scared. She'd been the one dealing with Mom, the twins, and a husband who traveled more than he was home. It was a lot for anyone to deal with on their own.

"I'm sorry, Lizzie." Meghan got up from the table and pulled her into a hug. It was only going to be worse when she found out that Meghan was heading for the middle east as soon as she could make the arrangements. She contemplated keeping it a secret until she got back with Charlie, but there's no way her sister would let her out of her sight without checking on her constantly.

"Go eat, it'll get cold."

"You are a great mom, Lizzie. And you're doing a hell of a job taking care of everything. I don't tell you that enough." From the surprised look on her face, she definitely didn't tell her enough.

111

"Keep that up and I'm going to be a total mess. What's going on? You're up to something."

"No. Nothing, at least not yet. I'm just trying to find out where Charlie is. And what we can do to get him back."

Lizzie gave her the side-eye. "Meggy, I can see right through you..."

"Seriously, that's all that's going on, for now."

"Ah, that's it. The infamous 'for now.' C'mon fess up or I'll sic Mom on you." It had been the ultimate threat when they were kids, and it had the same effect over twenty years later. No one wanted Mom involved in this.

"Fine, but nothing is settled. I'm going to go to Afghanistan. I need to do something."

"Are you out of your freaking mind?" Lizzie's voice came out high-pitched and furious. Slamming her hands on the table, she stood up and turned toward the window then turned back. "You are not going."

"Shh, you'll wake the twins."

"Meghan, promise me. You can't go. I won't lose both of my siblings to those maniacs."

"I can't make that promise. I need to do this. For Charlie, for all of us. But so far, I haven't figured out how to get the clearance. I'm hoping that Rafe's friend Tex will be able to help."

"And what about Rafe? He's okay with your little excursion into a war zone? Face it, if missionaries aren't safe, what makes you think you'll come back alive?"

"I have a plan, and I have to try. I can't just sit here and do nothing. Journalists go in and out of there all the time. I'm going to use that as cover and see if I can get them to give me an interview."

Lizzie opened the cabinet, grabbed a bottle of scotch and came back to the table with two glasses. "I don't know about you, but I need a drink. I think you've lost your ever-loving mind."

"I'll be fine, Lizzie. I promise I will."

"You can't make that promise." She was right, she really couldn't. It was dangerous, and maybe reckless, but she had to try. It was their baby brother and a bunch of other people who were only there to help others.

"To answer your question about Rafe, he doesn't know. He's been sent on a mission and no I don't know where. That's why he gave me his friend's contact information."

"Answer this. If he wasn't on a mission, would you still be trying to do this?"

Meghan thought about it for a bit. He wouldn't like it any more than Lizzie did, but the reasons for going wouldn't change. If he loved her the way he said, then he'd have to understand.

"Yes. I absolutely would. It would probably be harder because I wouldn't have his friend's information."

"And his friend is going to help you?"

"I don't know yet. I haven't talked to him."

"Maybe he'll say no."

"I suppose he might. Then I'll just have to find another way."

"You're gonna be the death of me. You and Charlie both. You're crazy, you know that?"

"Maybe. But traveling the world covering stories is what I've dreamed of doing my whole life. I'd be doing it anyway if I didn't work with a bunch of egotistical jerks. I can do this. I know it."

Lizzie shook her head and looked up at the ceiling. Then she poured another round of scotch. "I pray the good Lord watches over you, and you come back to us in one piece."

"I will." It had been hard for her to say those words. They both knew it, and Meghan would do her best to keep her promise.

"You ready for dessert?"

Meghan wasn't sure she could eat anything else. She'd been so hungry but now it was sitting like a lead weight in her stomach. Lizzie had taken the time to make it, so she'd eat it, somehow.

"Of course. You teased me with it, I can't wait." White lies aren't really bad, she told herself. The last thing she wanted was to piss off the big guy upstairs before she took this trip.

Lizzie but a plate in front of her with a huge slice of pie.

"You made lemon meringue pie for me?"

"Yup. I figured why not. What're a few calories

114

between sisters?" It was Meghan's favorite pie of all time but as she put the first forkful in her mouth it tasted like sawdust. But she'd hurt her sister enough already and bite by bite she ate every bit until her plate was empty.

"It was delicious." Ugh, another white lie. But it probably wouldn't have been if she hadn't begun second-guessing herself because of Lizzie's argument. Nope, she was going. With or without Tex's help.

"Since I can't talk you out of going, what's your plan. I need to know everything. So don't even try to hold anything back."

"I don't know everything. How about we call Tex together and see if he'll help?"

"It's the first idea you've had that I actually like. Imagine that?" Meghan smiled and squeezed Lizzie's hand. They'd all get through this and be stronger when it was over.

Dialing Tex's number, she pushed the button to put it on speaker and set it on the table between them.

"Tex."

"Hi. My name is Meghan Henley. I'm a friend of Rafe Buchanan's and he gave me your number. I hope it's okay to call?"

"Hi, Meghan. Rafe told me all about you. Is everything okay?"

"Yes. Well as much as it can be, I suppose. Oh, you're on speaker. My sister is here with me."

"Hi, Lizzie. How are you holding up?" The look on her face was priceless. She pointed to the phone and mouthed the words 'how does he know my name.'

"She's a little surprised right now. Rafe told me you were good."

"He has no idea. Sorry, I didn't mean to freak you out. When Rafe asked me to look into your brother's disappearance, I did research on all of you. I needed to make sure that their kidnapping wasn't because of anything he might be involved in at home."

"Our brother wouldn't do anything like that." Lizzie's voice vibrated in outrage.

"Hold on there, I wasn't implying that. I need to know everything."

"Lizzie. Please. He's helping us, right?"

"I guess. Sorry."

"No need to apologize, ma'am. I didn't mean to set you off. Just trying to explain. I swear, I'm on your side."

Meghan sure hoped so, because she didn't think he would be happy with her request.

"I have a favor to ask and I hope you can help me."

"What do you need. If I can help with it, I will."

"You may be sorry you said that here in a few minutes." Damn, she could hear her accent coming out. Stress was not her friend.

"Try me."

"Okay. I want to go to Afghanistan. Specifically, Bamyan Province to try to get my brother back."

Silence, if she hadn't heard his breathing, she'd swear he either keeled over from shock, or he'd hung up on her.

"Now I know why Rafe calls you spitfire."

"He calls you what? Lizzie asked.

"Spitfire." It was probably shock, but Lizzie started giggling and couldn't stop and it was contagious. Soon they were all laughing.

"He may have just met you, but dang he has you pinned," she replied as her giggles died off. "I am afraid to find out what made him call you that."

"I don't know. I guess you'll have to ask him when you meet him."

"I guess I will."

"Excuse me," Tex cut in. "Do you know how unsafe it is for anyone, let alone a single female to travel in Afghanistan?"

"Yes. I do. But I'm a journalist. It's my job to cover stories."

"You cover the society page and obits. That's not exactly a foreign correspondent job."

"That's true. But it's not for lack of trying. If I can pull this off, I'll get Charlie back and maybe even prove myself to my boss."

"You're willing to risk your life?"

"It's my brother. Wouldn't you?"

"Yes, but…"

"Don't you go telling me you're a man and it's safer."

"I was going to say I was a SEAL and trained for this."

Meghan sighed. Maybe she really had earned that nickname. "I'm sorry. I'm just so tired of being told I'm a woman so I can't or shouldn't do that."

"You need to help her, John."

"Meghan, Lizzie, that voice you hear is my wife, Melody."

"Mel. And I'm sorry for eavesdropping but I heard John laughing, so I came to investigate."

"Nice to meet you, Mel. I'm sorry I'm bothering your husband on a Saturday night."

"We're used to it. You have no idea how often this happens. No worries. I'm really sorry about your brother."

"Thank you. We appreciate that."

"I'll leave you all to work it out. Be careful Meghan. It's going to be a lot harder than you think."

"I will."

The phone was muffled for a few moments as Tex or John and Mel discussed something. Then he was back.

"John is my given name in case you were wondering. Tex is my name from the teams. I answer to either."

"I wondered. So, will you help me get to Afghanistan?"

"Rafe is going to kill me, but yes I will. You need to promise to follow the rules."

"What rules?"

"I'll spell them out for you before you leave. Monday look for a package from me. It will be a new phone with a tracking device. This way I can keep an eye on you while you're away."

"You can do that?"

"Oh yeah. That's nothing. Do you have a passport?"

"Yes. And yes, it's current.

"Good. Do you have credentials for your paper? Press passes?"

"Yes. I do."

"That'll make things easier. Okay, hang tight while I see what I can come up with. I'd suggest you pack for winter. It'll be cool and cold at night. Muted colors, nothing bright. You don't want to stand out, trust me."

"I will go shopping tomorrow."

"As soon as I have more information, I'll be in touch. If something changes in the interim text or call."

"I will. Thank you. I really appreciate all you've done for us."

"It's not that much. Yet. I just hope Rafe doesn't tan my hide when he gets back."

"Do you know where he is?"

"Yes, but I can't tell you."

"I figured. I only asked because I was wondering

just how far your reach went. I guess there's not much that can be hidden from you."

"You got that right. Anything else?"

"No. That's it. Thank you again."

"I'll be in touch. Bye."

"Holy crap, Meghan. I was praying he wouldn't help."

"It'll be okay, Lizzie."

"It better be."

Meghan smiled at her sister. When she was younger, she'd hated being the oldest child. But when she grew up and eventually moved out on her own, it changed, and she actually missed being around them all the time.

"How do the kids like the mall?"

"Lia loves it, CJ not so much. But it'll be fine. I don't think bringing Mom is a good idea though. I'll get one of the aides to come over."

"Probably a good idea."

CHAPTER 11

The team landed at Bagram Air Force Base in Afghanistan just before sunrise. They were supposed to have all the intel on where the hostages were held, but they didn't. Lynch's people hadn't gotten positive confirmation of their location or even which tribe had them. Captain Knox contacted Command and they were told to stand down. They were worried that if the team headed out without verification of where the HVT was they would end up causing her death. Apparently, the Senator and the President were close friends.

The base was bustling with early morning activity. Rafe was so keyed up there was no way he'd be able to get any shut-eye. What he wanted to do was talk to Meghan. He had a bad feeling that something was wrong, and it wasn't going away. He needed to hear her voice, but he'd settle for a text message. But with a nine and a half hour time difference, it was after midnight back in Atlanta. Too late to call and he didn't want to take a chance he'd wake her with a text message. The other option was Tex, but it was even later there, and Jake had told him to disengage. He couldn't disobey a direct order.

That left only one thing, going for a run. He'd burn off the excess energy and maybe be able to rest finally. After dumping his pack in their temporary quarters, he grabbed a bottle of water.

"Where are you going?" Jake asked.

"For a run. I can't sit here and do nothing."

Jake nodded. "No problem. Don't go too far in case they actually come up with some intel we can use."

"Copy that."

"Want company?" Ryan asked.

"Sure."

"We won't be long, Boss."

"Catch you when you get back."

They left the tent and headed for the outskirts of the base to run the perimeter of the airfield. Bagram was practically a second home to the team, having been there more times than they could count. Neither of the men spoke as they circled the airfield. The breeze picked up as the sun rose over the horizon. It was fall and the desert air was cool, but the dry air eventually forced them to stop and hydrate. They knew better than to get dehydrated.

"What's got you so hot and bothered?" Ryan asked after taking a swig from his water bottle.

"This mission."

"Don't give me that bullshit. Crappy intel happens on almost every mission. It's more the norm than not."

"True that. But I met a woman the other day and her brother is one of the hostages."

"No fucking way."

"I wish it wasn't. When I went to stay with Dawn and the kids, I got stuck in the airport. I'd been watching her for a while but couldn't decide if I wanted to take the chance that she would be one of those women like we deal with in the bar all the time. But after the flight got canceled and I heard her spout a list of cuss words that would have shocked you, I couldn't resist."

"I take it she wasn't after you for your cute SEAL ass?"

"Hell no. At first, I didn't think she would even respond. She mellowed as the wait went on."

"I bet she did."

"No, it wasn't like that at all. She didn't even ask what I did in the Navy. If I hadn't volunteered it, she wouldn't have known I was a SEAL."

"Why did you?"

"Probably because she didn't ask. She didn't even ask for my name. I had to volunteer that, and it was only after she'd seen the news about her brother. If that hadn't happened, I don't think it would have gone any further."

Rafe would have gone on but a C-130 came in for a landing. The roar of the engines made it impossible to hear anything and vibrated the ground where they stood. It taxied down the runway and came to a stop on the other side of the airfield, bringing in the next group of troops and replenishing supplies.

"It's not like you to talk to female strangers. In fact, it's the exact opposite of you. Cam? Murph? Sure, but you? No fucking way."

"I know. But there was something about her. She's a little ball of fire wrapped up in a body to kill for. If she's five foot it's a lot, but damn she's got curves in all the right places. You know? A woman you can hold on to and not worry about breaking."

Ryan nodded but didn't respond. There was a gleam in his eyes that warned Rafe that trouble was coming.

"She has long black hair, the most expressive green-blue eyes I've ever seen, and the cutest smattering of freckles along her cheekbones."

"Shit, bro. You've got it bad."

"Right? I don't know what the fuck happened. It's like she cast a spell on me."

"Or you finally met your one. It's what we're all inherently craving."

"What the fuck are you talking about?"

"Philosophy, dude. You know Plato, right?"

124

"Yeah. What does he have to do with this?"

"In the book *The Symposium*, he wrote that according to Greek Mythology humans were originally created with four arms, four legs, and a head with two faces. But Zeus was afraid of their power and split them into two separate parts. Now we spend our lifetimes searching for our other half so we can be whole again."

"How the fuck do you know this shit?"

"I read a lot and I happen to love philosophy."

"So, is that where the soul mate thing comes from?"

"Probably."

"I guess I learned something new. Go figure." It made as much sense as anything else in the fucked up world. Ryan was right about one thing, he was the last one of the team to approach a woman. There were plenty who hounded him and the rest of the team, but it wasn't what he was looking for. He wanted what his parents had, what Dawn had with Bob. Up until he met Meghan, he didn't think it was possible.

They continued their trek around the airfield at a slower pace so they could continue their conversation.

"She was lucky to have you there when she found out."

"I'm not sure she thinks so. But I tell you, she didn't even lose it."

"No tears?"

"Not at first. She was in shock, sure. But she held it together. Trying to figure out how to get him back."

"I'm impressed."

"Yeah, so was I. That's why I had to bring Tex into it."

"Makes sense to me. Besides, it wasn't our mission yet."

"Exactly. And since it wasn't, I couldn't ask Jake to get me intel either. That only left Tex and his amazing computer super powers."

"I'm sure she appreciated your help."

"Yes, until she found out I hadn't told her everything. Once Tex found out he was definitely one of the hostages, I kept it from her at first. She got so pissed off she lost it, and that's when the tears came. Then she chewed my ass a new one, but she was so quiet Jake would have been proud. But I deserved it."

"You were only trying to protect her…"

"That's what I thought, but she didn't see it that way. To her, I was hiding information from her about her family, information I'd promised to get for her."

"Did Tex find out anything else?"

"Yeah, that the senator's daughter was part of the missionary group. Hell, I think he knew it before the state department."

Ryan chuckled. "Probably did. The man knows everything."

"That's what I told Meghan. When we got called in, I gave her his information in case she needed anything."

"Good plan. He'll be able to keep her updated since you can't."

"Yeah. But when Jake found out he told me no more contact with Tex."

"What did you expect him to say?"

"I know, but I can't shake this feeling that Meghan is in trouble."

"Where did you leave her?"

"In Atlanta at her sister's house."

"I'm sure she's fine there."

"Hope so. I'd call but it's too damn late."

"And that's why we're running, huh?"

"Yup. You got it."

"Guess we better get on with it. I'll race you back."

Running full out was just what Rafe needed to burn off the rest of his pent-up tension. By the time they got back to the tent sleep sounded good, but first he needed to wash off the grit from the blowing sand.

Bill Lynch and Jake were in the middle of a heated discussion as he approached their tent. The fury on Jake's face didn't bode well for Bill, and his gut clenched with worry for the hostages. He'd hoped to hear something, but their conversation stopped as soon as he approached.

"Any news?"

"Not what we wanted," Jake answered.

"They're in the mountains about twenty klicks from the village where they were grabbed," Bill added.

"What's the problem. We go in and get them, no?"

"They know about Miranda Stanhope."

"Fuck." They'd hoped to keep that information quiet. Most likely one of the other hostages said something hoping to help themselves. Not that you could blame them. They were probably terrified.

Bill nodded and continued, "This is where it gets dicey. Our intel says they've separated them. They still plan to sell the main group for arms. But now they're demanding a prisoner exchange and money for the HVT."

The grim expression on Jake's face said it all. He also knew that Rafe had even more reason to want to rescue the other hostages. Their primary mission would be to recover Miranda Stanhope. The other hostages would be secondary if they were told to do it at all.

Sleep was no longer an option. Fear and fury warred within Rafe but instead of losing it, his training took over. One of his strengths was problem solving, running scenarios in his head until he'd found a solution. If there was a way to save them all, with or without permission, he'd find it. The only positive in any of this was that he couldn't tell Meghan. His little spitfire would've had a nuclear meltdown, and he wouldn't have blamed her. Rescuing all of them was the only option, whether JSOC agreed or not.

"Rafe, did you hear me?"

"Huh?"

"That's what I thought. TOC now."

"Copy that."

ONCE THEY WERE GATHERED in the Tactical Operations Center, Bill signed in to the video transmission from Joint Special Operations Command. An hour later they had their mission plan, the direction had come from the president, and there was no arguing with the commander-in-chief. Orders were orders. It sucked that they'd have to wait two days to go get her. But JSOC wanted proof of life and double confirmation of her location before they went in to do the rescue. Rafe prayed that the mission to save Miranda Stanhope didn't mean a death sentence for the rest of the hostages.

After the briefing with JSOC was finished, Captain Knox continued with the specifics, going over maps and locations until they had their plan nailed down.

"You'll helo in at oh-one hundred. If they haven't moved her, it'll be about fifteen klicks to the HVT. You need to be at the EXFIL at oh-five-hundred," Captain Knox finished. "Any questions?"

"No, sir," Jake responded for all of them. None of them were happy, from the captain on down. Their only option was to rescue Miranda and take out her captors before they could alert the others. And if they had good intel on where the other hostages were being held, they should be able to free them before it was too late. There were a lot of 'if's' in the equation, but it wasn't the worst plan they'd ever had to execute.

"I don't like this, Boss," Rafe said so only Jake could hear him.

"It doesn't matter. You know the drill. It's not the first double extraction we've done. It won't be our last."

"Usually they're in the same location. We're not even sure where the other hostages are being held."

"Rafe, I know you've never been personally invested before, but these are our orders. Is this a problem?"

"No, sir." Jake was right, he needed to get his head on straight. This was what they did, what they trained for every fucking day.

Back at their tent, they went over the maps, searched the terrain and re-read the reports. As tired as he had been, Rafe didn't rest until late afternoon when his body didn't give him a choice.

A wet tongue woke him too soon. He'd been dreaming about Meghan and didn't appreciate Halo licking him awake. "What the fuck, man?"

"Jake sent me to wake you for dinner, bro.

Unless you'd rather have an MRE?" Cam answered, but all he saw was the teeth and tongue of his furry teammate.

"Fuck, no."

"Then you owe Halo an apology."

Cam was right. "Thanks, boy." He swore the dog smiled at him before trotting after Cam. Rubbing the sleep off his face, he checked the time and did some quick calculations. It was eight thirty a.m. in Atlanta. Way too early to call, but not to text. Texting would definitely be safer. There were too many things he couldn't share with her, but he didn't want to go dark without at least checking that she was okay. It might be a while before he had another chance. After typing and deleting a message three different times, he finally settled on brief, simple, and to the point. Then he clicked send.

Hey Spitfire. Stay positive. I'll text when I can. Love you, Rafe

It didn't take long to get a response. He hadn't gotten halfway to the Mess when the phone vibrated in his pocket.

All good here. Tex is great. Be safe, big guy. Love, Meg

Maybe he'd worried for nothing. He'd know for sure if he could hear her voice, but he'd have to settle for her words for now. Besides, if something happened Tex knew how to get ahold of him.

CHAPTER 12

True to his word, Tex arranged everything. All she had to do was pack and make sure she had a valid Press ID, although he probably could have come up with one of those too. So far, she had the easy part, but what was coming would take all the strength and determination she had to get through. After Tex's warning that the hostages may have been tortured, she'd almost reconsidered the plan. Almost. The thought of her brother being beaten, or worse, was horrifying, but it also strengthened her resolve to get him home.

It had been two days since Rafe, and his team had left for wherever. She'd only heard from him once. It would be driving her up the wall with worry if she hadn't been planning her own excursion. He'd be madder than a bull when he found out, but with any luck, it wouldn't be until she was back home safe and sound with her brother.

The phone rang as she was putting the last of her clothes in the suitcase. Expecting it to be Tex she didn't check the caller ID.

"Hey, are we all set?"

"I'm not sure what you mean." Dang it. She really needed to be more careful.

"Excuse me. I thought you were someone else."

"Obviously. I'm Ted Clement from the state department. I'm returning your call." It took him long enough, she'd left him the message almost three days ago.

"Thank you for calling me back. We were hoping you'd have news about our brother." Too bad for him that she already had all the information there was courtesy of Tex. But it would be interesting to see if he lied to her or not.

"We don't really have anything new. There haven't been any demands made by the kidnappers."

"Don't you mean the terrorists?" Meghan tried to restrain her temper but if he was going to continue to feed her manure, she was going to lose it.

"I'm sorry, Ms. Henley. But that's all the information I have." After taking a deep breath, she answered with all the southern charm she could shove into one sentence.

"Well bless your little heart, I'm sure that's all they told you to tell us poor families as we worry ourselves sick. But it's just cruel to keep us in the dark."

"I assure you..."

"I'm sure you do. But you can be assured that I'll be contacting your superior and moving up the food chain until we find out the truth about our brother. Now you have a nice day, you hear?" Without waiting for his reply, she disconnected the call and had to stop herself from throwing the phone against the wall. What a sorry piece of shit. To think that her tax dollars paid his salary and he couldn't even tell her the truth.

She'd been truly blessed when she and Rafe connected, and even more so when he gave her the means to help her brother. The next time the phone rang she checked the number before answering, but it wasn't one she recognized.

"Hello."

"Meghan? It's Tex. Sorry but I'm sure they are probably tracking your number so I'm using a burner."

"Who is?"

"The state department, the CIA, any one of the alphabet agencies. It would make sense that they'd monitor all the families."

"Oh. But what about before?"

"It was routed through my computer and through so many countries they'd have a hard time tracking me."

"I'm not sure I get all this cloak and dagger stuff."

"It's okay. It's better if you don't get mixed up in it anyway," he answered with a chuckle. It made her wonder what he was like in person. She knew he had a wife, Mel. But what was he really like? Was he like a spy out of a movie?

"Your new phone should arrive today. There will be extra SIM cards in the box. They're for overseas so you can call me, your sister, and make the calls you need to while in Afghanistan. If you call home, make sure to destroy the SIM card before you make any more calls. Got it?"

"Yup. Destroy cards between calls home."

"The sooner the better, okay?"

"Okay. Do you really think they'll be tracking me?"

"Yes, I do. But maybe I'm just paranoid." Another chuckle eased some of the tension that had been churning in her belly. Maybe she was out of her mind trying to do this on her own.

"Yeah, I don't think so."

"Good. Because it never hurts to be extra careful."

"I understand. I know what I'm doing might be considered crazy, but I can't just sit here while everyone gives us the runaround and my brother is out there hurt or worse."

"I think you're a brave woman, maybe a tad

crazy. I wouldn't want my wife doing what you're about to. Rafe is going to have my head on a silver platter too. But I think you might have a chance as long as the Taliban don't find out you're related to one of the hostages."

"I figured that. I got all the supplies you sent in the email, all the head coverings too."

"Good. We just have to hope if you see your brother that he doesn't blow your cover."

"I know. But after all the different options we considered I still think this is the best."

"I just emailed your flight information and your VISA. Make sure you memorize your cover story. I'll check on Lizzie while you're out of the country."

"Thank you, Tex. For everything."

"Don't thank me yet. Save that for when you get back. Stick to the plan, check in on schedule and send the SOS if things go sideways."

"I will."

"Bye, Meghan. Be safe."

"Thanks. I will." After she disconnected the call, she dropped onto the bed. Staring up at the ceiling, she replayed Tex's words. He'd been there, fought there, knew his way around and had connections. As long as his information was correct about where her brother was being held, she'd be fine. She had to be. All of her research into the Taliban over the last twenty-four hours would help too. They had a solid plan, she'd follow the instructions Tex had given her and carry out her mission. There was no room for failure.

THIRTY HOURS LATER, her plane touched down at Kabul International Airport. It had been a long flight via Turkey, but she'd made it. Tex had gotten her there in one piece. But now she was on her own. Her press pass and the Visa that he'd secured got her through customs without an issue. As she made her way through the airport, she couldn't shake the feeling she was being watched. It might have just been her imagination, but she'd swear that there were two men tailing her. She was a female traveling alone and definitely out of place with her western attire, but she'd prepared for that as well.

Pulling out her phone, she checked for messages, happy to see there weren't any. No message meant no changes. Acquiring transportation to Bamyan was the next part of her plan. She'd start from the village where the group had been working to build the school. But first, she really needed to use the bathroom. Finally, she located the universal sign for restroom. Praying it wasn't going to be weird, she was relieved to find the usual facilities. After washing up the best she could, she pulled out one of the hijabs from her bag and draped it over her head then wrapped it around her neck and shoulders. Tex assured her that it would be sufficient and that no one would expect her to wear a burqa.

After checking the mirror one last time to ensure her hair was covered properly, an image of Rafe flashed into her head. "Oh man, if he could see me now, I'd have my ass in a sling." Just thinking about it almost made her laugh, but not quite. She wasn't out of her mind, was she?

If it had been that bad, Tex would have talked her out of it. Or Lizzie would have, yet neither had put up much of a fight when she'd told them her plan. Instead, they'd all worked together to finesse all the arrangements until it was as close to perfect as possible. Now she just needed to stick to it, and that required she find transportation for the one hundred kilometer trip to the village.

After taking a deep breath and settling her pack on her shoulders, she made her way to the airport exit. Busier than expected, Tex told her to look for a bus rather than a taxi, that it would be safer, but there were taxis everywhere. Not sure when the next bus would come, or if there was a direct one to Bamyan, she debated on whether to chance grabbing one of the taxis anyway.

"Excuse me, are you Meghan Henley?" A deep British voice asked from behind her left shoulder. It startled her to hear her name.

"Yes," she answered as she turned to face him, ready to run back into the airport terminal depending on what he did next. "Who are you and how do you know my name?" The man was medium height and average build and would blend in anywhere, there was absolutely nothing that made him stand out except for his accent.

"I apologize for startling you. My name is James Waltham. Your friend Tex said you might need a ride?"

"You know Tex?"

"I do. He contacted me last night and asked if I had time to take you on a tour of the countryside."

"A tour?" She wished she could verify it with Tex. Why hadn't he told her or sent her a message? Maybe he hadn't thought it was necessary, or maybe she was walking into a trap. "I'm not sure." She really wasn't.

Waltham grabbed her by the elbow and led her away from the crowds exiting the terminal. She felt like a fish out of water and wasn't sure what to believe. "I am sure you are concerned about my credentials," he said as he pulled out his wallet and opened it to show her his license and his name badge. "Didn't Tex tell you I would be meeting you?"

"No, he didn't. I checked my messages when I arrived and there was nothing. He grunted and she took a step back, making sure she had enough room to dart around him if she needed to. The years of Zumba classes might finally come in handy. She was about to say thanks no thanks when her pocket vibrated. Watching him carefully, she slipped her phone out and glanced at it. The text message appeared on the screen.

Sent help for your trip. James is qualified and you can trust him. Tex.

Her relief was tangible as she re-read the message. "Actually, it looks like he did. Maybe it was delayed since my phone was off."

Waltham smiled. "Now that's settled, are you ready to go? It's about a three hour trip."

"Three? It's only a bit over one hundred kilometers."

"Yes, but you're not in the states, it's slow and can be dangerous. But I promised Tex I'd make sure you got there safely."

"Why did he send someone from the British Embassy and not an American?"

He quirked an eyebrow before answering. "I think you already know the answer to that. They have to report that you're here. You wouldn't have gotten further than the sidewalk outside of the arrival terminal."

It made perfect sense when he said it. She was tired, stressed and a little hungry. It would have been smart if she'd bought something to eat while she was inside the airport.

"My jeep is in the side parking lot, just around the corner there. I packed some food and extra supplies since there won't be many places to stop along the way."

"Thanks, I appreciate it."

"When Tex first told me that I would need to take someone to Bamyan, I didn't expect it to be a woman. You've got a set of bollocks on you, I'll give you that. Traveling all alone to a war zone to interview the Taliban. Impressive."

"I'm not exactly alone though, am I? You'll be with me."

"At least as far as Bamyan. I won't be able to stay."

Tex must not have told him the real reason she'd come. It was fine with her and she had no plans on enlightening him either. Rafe told her she could trust Tex and she'd put her life in his hands. It didn't mean she had to trust anyone else. There was something off about Waltham. Just standing near him raised the little hairs on the back of her neck, and her sister's words to her niece, 'stranger danger' echoed in her head.

Not one bus had stopped or even driven by the front of the terminal. There were no indications that situation would change anytime soon so traveling with Waltham or hiring one of the random taxi drivers standing around were her only options. Waltham seemed like a better choice. If Tex sent him, and she had to believe he had, then he'd know where to look if something happened to her.

"Have you changed your mind? I wouldn't blame you if you do," Waltham said as he studied her face.

"No, I haven't changed my mind. Let's go." She'd held off long enough, it was time to pull up her big girl panties and do what she'd come there to do. Whispering a prayer that she'd be able to pull this off, she followed Waltham to his car.

CHAPTER 13

It was go time. The semi-silent whoosh of the helicopter blades cut through the darkness. There was nothing as black as the middle of the night in the desert. The only light was from the stars in the sky and what was left of the moon, once they were out of range of Bagram.

They were all silent, each member of the team reviewed their part of the plan. Running scenarios in their mind to cover the unexpected. They were in a war zone, it was anticipated. Chances are plan A would become plan B or C before they even headed back to base. Rafe had never been on a mission where at least one thing hadn't gone sideways in the worst way possible. It was part of the process, and because of that, they tried to imagine every possible variable.

As they neared the drop off point, the mood on the chopper changed, grew more focused, intense, battle ready. But it was really just years of training and preparation. Jake nodded at each one of his teammates and ran the com check. While on missions, they went by their team position. Jake was Master Chief and Eagle 1, he was Eagle 2, Ryan was Eagle 3, Murph was Eagle 4, and Cam was Eagle 5.

Seconds later, they were on the ground, night vision on, alert for anything out of the ordinary as they blended into the silent world around them. Like ghosts, they moved through the night.

A half hour later they'd arrived at the first checkpoint. They'd been able to move quickly over the rocky terrain and hadn't come across anyone. Jake was talking to TOC while the team waited to hear if there had been any new intel.

Halo calmly sniffed around them while Rafe's eyes were constantly moving, searching for anything out of the ordinary. Then his com whispered in his ear. "We have confirmation on the location of HVT. No changes."

"Copy that, Eagle 1," Rafe replied.

"We should make the next checkpoint in thirty mikes." It was peaceful, too peaceful. Rafe didn't like it. Even though it was mountainous terrain, there should have been animal sounds. There is always something, but all he heard was their boots on the ground.

"Eagle 1, it's too quiet."

"Agreed. Eagle 5, Halo picking up anything?"

The dog usually ran at the front and was their first warning if anything was out of place.

"Nothing, Eagle 1. It's like they knew we were coming."

Rafe had the same feeling. It was going way too smoothly. Sad, but true. There had to be something. Jake signaled for them to stop and echoed the command in their coms.

"TOC, this is Eagle 1."

"Go ahead, Eagle 1."

"It's too quiet. Are you seeing anything?"

"Copy that, Eagle 1. The drone should be in range in a few minutes. Stand by."

"TOC, we're on the move to checkpoint blue. Don't want to get behind."

"Copy that. We'll advise when we have visual."

They moved with purpose but care, anticipating anything from an ambush to land mines. They'd made it out alive of every previous mission because they watched each other's six and were careful.

It was almost three klicks before they heard back from TOC. The captain didn't sound happy either. "Eagle 1?"

Again, Jake signaled for them to stop. "'TOC, this is Eagle 1."

"Eagle 1, be advised there are at least ten tangos within two klicks of your location."

Now they had to wonder if it was a standard patrol or if they'd been alerted that they were coming. If they knew, had they moved Miranda

Stanhope? If she'd been moved this had been a complete waste of time and resources.

"Copy that, TOC. We'll proceed with caution."

"You heard the captain, we're close to the next checkpoint which should be within a klick of where they're holding the hostage." Jake pulled out his map and laid it on the rocky ground. "Eagle 3 and 4, I want you to circle around through here, Eagle 5 keep on the current track. Eagle 2 and I will go to the left through this pass here."

They nodded and silently disappeared into the blackness. They'd meet at the checkpoint and see what they were dealing with when they got there. It would have to be a quick in and out with only two hours left until they had to be at the EXFIL point with Miranda.

Jake and Rafe moved stealthily through the brush, knives in one hand and guns in the other. As they approached the checkpoint, they saw at least four heavily armed enemy combatants guarding the cave where Miranda was being held.

"Do you see what I'm seeing?" Rafe whispered.

"Yes. Hopefully, it means HVT is still at this location," Jake replied, and Rafe nodded. "Eagle 3, sitrep?"

"Eagle 3 at checkpoint."

"Eagle 5, sitrep?"

"Eagle 5 at overlook. Four tangos visible."

"Copy that Eagle 5."

Rafe pulled out his binoculars to get a closer

look. If they were expecting company, they were stupid. A raging fire burned near the entrance to the cave. Besides the four tangos standing, he could see at least three more inside the mouth of the cave.

"Three more tangos inside."

"Where are the other three? TOC reported ten," Jake asked.

Rafe didn't like it. Were they further in the cave with Miranda?

"What do you want to do, Boss," Rafe asked as he squatted next to Jake. They had a clear view of the cave entrance, Ryan and Murph were also within range. The four of them could easily take out the seven Taliban soldiers. But they didn't know who or what was waiting for them inside the cave.

"TOC, this is Eagle 1."

"Go ahead, Eagle 1."

"We're at the final checkpoint. We confirm seven tangos."

"Eagle 1, the last drone pass confirmed ten."

"Copy that, TOC. We'll send Halo to check out the cave."

"Copy that, Eagle 1. You have ninety minutes to get to EXFIL. Once the sun's up, we can't get you."

"Copy that."

"Eagle 5, make your way to Eagle 3's location. Send Halo in."

"Copy, Eagle 1."

Rafe would have made the same call. Jake was

smart and careful. Halo had a camera and they'd be able to see what he saw, and hopefully without being noticed.

As he continued to monitor the guard's location through the binoculars, he watched Halo slip past two of them and enter the cave. Cam would be watching the progress on his tablet and reporting. But so far, no movement on the outside. A few minutes later Cam's voice came over their coms.

"Eagle 1, we have confirmation of HVT."

"Does she look injured?"

"She's been beaten. They have her tied to a chair with a blanket or something wrapped around her. I can't tell if she's wired."

"Copy that."

The Taliban were known for booby-trapping their hostages because of missions like this. Murph could disarm anything if he had enough time, the one thing they didn't have to spare. Jake's mind worked a lot like his, so he knew that he was deciding on the best option for the breach.

The guards looked restless. It could mean they were waiting for their relief or they were expecting the SEALs. If it was the latter, they wouldn't have to wait for long. Finally, Halo slipped back out of the cave's opening and made his way to Cam.

"Eagle 3 and 4 take out the guards, then follow us in. Remember, once we get inside, we need at least one of the tangos alive. We'll grab HVT and head to EXFIL."

"Copy, Boss."

"We go in three."

SEALs were quick and deadly, and their team was one of the best. As Rafe and Jake approached the cave, Murph and Ryan had already taken out the four tangos and had them on the ground. Jake led the way with Halo and the others at his heels. The five men moved swiftly following the sounds of conversation and flickering light.

The men holding Miranda never even knew they were there until it was too late. They'd taken out three before their leader realized what was happening. The SEALs expected them to put up more of a fight. The whole thing seemed off and made the back of Rafe's neck tingle.

"I don't like this, Boss. It was too fuckin' easy."

"Agreed. Maybe we just got lucky." None of them believed it. Once they got the information they needed from the leader, they'd get the hell out of there. They hadn't needed to fire a shot.

While Jake, Ryan, and Murph questioned the leader who was shrieking in Pashto, Rafe and Cam went to release Miranda. Her captor's put her in a chair out of hearing range of their conversation. It was common practice, but Rafe doubted the senator's daughter spoke let alone understood the Afghani language. It was also the coldest, dampest part of the cavern.

As they approached her, the injuries she'd sustained were more evident. Her busted lip and bruised cheeks filled him with rage. He'd never understand how men could beat women. Clenching his fists, he ached to go back and kill the men all over again as punishment for what they'd done to her.

They weren't sure how much she'd heard, or understood, of what had gone on since she was blindfolded. Rafe expected to hear her crying or whimpering in pain. Blindfolded and wrapped in some kind of dark cloth, there wasn't a sound coming from the woman. He and Cam exchanged glances, then he spoke softly as he reached out to her hoping to keep her calm.

"Miranda Stanhope? Are you Miranda Stanhope?"

At first, there was nothing, no answer, no movement at all and Rafe was worried that they'd done more damage to the young woman than they'd thought.

"We're here to take you home, Miranda. I know you've got to be scared, but we're here to help. I'm going to remove your blindfold. Close your eyes so you can get used to the light. Ready?"

Finally, she responded with a soft, "yes, sir." It was low pitched, but firm, no quivering. Considering her condition, that surprised him. As he removed the blindfold, he revealed a black eye and a long cut from her eyebrow to the outer corner of her right eye. Her left cheek was just one huge purple bruise. *Fucking bastards.*

"How much pain are you in?"

"I'm okay. I just want to go home." It was as if their presence finally sank in and she struggled to stand.

"Don't move, Miranda, we need to see what's under this blanket. You might be wired to something." Fear flooded into her face and make the bruises and dried blood stand out even more. Before Rafe could do anything to reassure her, Halo appeared at her side and wagged his tail. The dog was a godsend. "Okay, I'm going to slowly remove the wrap and then we'll know."

"Fuck," Cam said with a low whistle. It didn't help the situation but it sure as hell fit. It wasn't a full vest, but they'd rigged some kind of a wide belt around her waist what had C-4 and God knows what else. Rafe walked around to the back of the chair to see if they could move her at all, but it was attached to the chair rungs.

"Don't move, honey. We're going to get you out of this." She nodded. Without the blanket, Rafe checked her carefully for any other injuries. Her wrists were raw and bleeding from being tied too tightly to the chair. He wanted to cut her lose but he was afraid she wouldn't be able to stop herself from trying to stand.

"Do you remember them putting this on you?"

She shook her head no. "When we got here, a man asked me all kinds of questions. I didn't know the answers and he beat me. I don't remember passing out, but when I woke up, I was blindfolded and couldn't move."

"Do you see him here? Is he one of these men?"

She squinted and looked over at the three men leaning against the table. They were dead but their faces hadn't been destroyed. The leader was still yelling at Jake.

"I don't think so. He was different than them."

"Different, how?" Cam asked as his dog rubbed his head against her leg. It was about the only place not dripping blood.

Rafe tapped his com. "Murph, we need you." Time wasn't on their side and having to disarm the bomb before they could get her out of there made things more complicated. The odds of making their EXFIL were dwindling with every heartbeat.

Moments later, Murph knelt next to Miranda and examined the explosives. If there was a way to get it off her without it detonating, he'd find it. If they were lucky, the big guy shouting Pashto would tell them how to disarm it or at least the triggers. He was about to ask Jake when a gunshot echoed around the chamber. He turned in time to see the man tip back in his chair and hit the floor with a bullet through his forehead. It didn't look they'd get any assistance after all.

"What do you think, Murph?"

"It's not the worst I've seen but it's not going to be easy. And it's going to take a bit."

It wasn't what they wanted to hear, but you'd

never know from the looks on their faces. They needed to keep Miranda calm until they could get her loose. Jake joined them as Murph announced the good news.

"Miranda. I'm Jake, this is Rafe, Ryan is over there, Murph is working on getting you free so we can get out of here, and the guy with the dog is Cam."

"Thank you so much. I am so glad you're here. I thought they were going to kill me."

"That's not going to happen. We'll get you back home as soon as we can."

"What about the rest of my group? There were ten of us…"

"We know and we're working on a plan to rescue them too." They were? Last he knew their mission was to rescue Miranda and get her back to Bagram Air Force Base. Maybe Jake had spoken to TOC or he was just trying to keep her calm.

"Thank goodness. I was so worried something had happened to them."

"The information we have is that they are all together and okay. You were the only one separated. Do you know how they found out who you were?"

"I can't say for sure, but if I had to guess it was Richard. He was terrified when we were taken. He would have done just about anything to stay safe, and I can't blame him for that if he was the one."

"That's very understanding of you," Jake replied.

Rafe and he exchanged looks and he nodded and stepped away from them to call command. They needed as much information on Richard as possible. He might have been a plant, or it could have been as Miranda said, that he'd just been scared to death.

"TOC, this is Eagle 2."

"Go ahead, Eagle 2."

"We have HVT. Murph is diffusing the explosive belt before we can move her."

"Copy that. We also need more info on one of the missionary group. First name Richard."

"What are we looking for?"

"Not sure. Miranda thinks he might have been the one to share her identity with their captors."

"Copy that. We'll go through the list again."

"It doesn't look like we'll make it to the EXFIL point on time. We need a new plan."

"You're going to have to stay hidden until nightfall."

"Copy that. I'll advise Eagle 1." It's what they'd expected. It was too risky to try to fly the chopper in during daylight hours. If Jake had found out where the other hostages were being held, then maybe they could recover them all by sundown.

CHAPTER 14

Meghan was losing her mind listening to the endless ramblings of James Waltham. Until this trip, she'd been under the misconception that men didn't like small talk. Oh, how wrong she was. For the last hour and a half, she'd been cooped up in the jeep gazing at mile after mile of sand and listening to the world gold medal winner of chat. She didn't need to say a word, he managed to keep the conversation going with only an occasional comment from her.

So far, he'd discussed the sand, seasons, wildlife, and more than anyone in the world should know about tea. She hated tea. Despised it. It was practically sacrilegious being from the south and refusing to drink sweet tea. It was considered a birthright. But even if it had been a beverage she'd enjoyed, she'd never have drunk it again after this trip. The more he yammered the more her head pounded. She'd already popped an Advil, but it hadn't done much to relieve the pain.

Just when she thought she'd lose it, she realized he'd stopped talking. It was quiet. She turned from the window to make sure he was still alive. It was the first quiet in ages. Imagine that. He'd stopped to take a drink from his water bottle. But it would only be a matter of time before he started up again.

"How much longer until we get to Bamyan?"

"If things stay as they are, probably another hour or so." If she looked on the bright side, she was more than halfway there. But she couldn't hold in a groan when she thought about another hour of listening to his yakking.

"I thought Afghanistan was more populated than this."

"It depends on where you are. This area has seen a lot of fighting and so the villagers who were here have mostly moved on to other areas. With the blowing sand, it doesn't take long to erase a lot of what was once there."

That made sense and was useful information. Maybe she was being too hard on Waltham. If she asked more questions, she'd probably have learned more that would be helpful. It couldn't have been easy dropping everything and driving a stranger across a warzone. She'd never even asked what he did. When he'd said embassy, she just assumed he was some kind of spy since he knew Tex. She wasn't sure if he and Tex had worked together or were friends. Not that it mattered. The only thing that mattered was rescuing her brother. Or at the very least seeing for herself that he was alive.

"Bloody hell."

"What's wrong?" Meghan asked. She didn't see anything, but Waltham glanced between the rearview and side mirrors, and sweat beaded on his forehead before he pulled a ringing satellite phone out of the armrest. The reporters that traveled overseas for the paper had them, so they wouldn't have to worry about SIM cards or access. What was going on? His actions raised the hairs on the back of her neck. Nothing looked different but his whole demeanor had changed.

"Yes. I've got the girl. No. About an hour, but there's smoke ahead."

Smoke? She didn't see any smoke all she saw was blowing sand. Then she squinted and looked through the dusty windshield and saw what could have been a plume in the distance.

"Okay. Let me know." He disconnected the call and laid the phone in his lap. He'd slowed his speed, which hadn't been very fast to begin with, and sighed. "Looks like our luck may be changing. There's a skirmish up ahead."

"What does that mean for us?"

"It means we may not get to Bamyan tonight. Depending on what is happening and how close to the road it is, we may have to spend the night out here. Tex is trying to find out who and what is

159

going on. If it's the Americans, they'll most likely let us pass. If it is the Taliban or the Afghani forces, we'll need to stay as far away from it as possible."

"But I came here to meet with the Taliban."

"Not in the middle of a firefight you didn't." No, she didn't, but if it was the only way to find out about Charlie then so be it.

"I don't…"

"Just hold on to your britches. When Tex calls back we'll know more. For now, grab something for us to eat out of the cooler."

Waltham was treating her like a child, and it irked her. Meghan didn't want to eat but didn't see any point in objecting. She was in an unfamiliar country and in his car. He could make whatever rules he wanted. Reaching into the backseat, she grabbed a couple of sandwiches and two more bottles of water out of the cooler. As she closed the lid, she glanced through the back window.

"Oh shit. I think we have company," Meghan said as she settled into her seat.

"I saw them. Just follow my lead and it should fine."

"You keep saying that."

"Exactly, so you should listen to me."

Exhaustion and fear were making her cranky. None of this was Waltham's fault, he'd been nothing but kind, polite, and helpful. She'd probably still be waiting at the airport for a bus if it weren't for him.

"I'm sorry. I'm not usually like this."

"It's okay, just try to remain calm. Hopefully, they'll just keep going and leave us alone. But if they make us pull over don't make any sudden moves."

"Okay." Rafe was going to kill her if she made it back alive. The more this trip progressed the more she wondered if she'd been out of her mind. It didn't seem nearly as dangerous when she'd come up with the plan. News reporters traveled in and out of Afghanistan all the time and nothing happened. But they also weren't chasing down kidnappers. She started to wonder if the only reason Tex helped her was to make sure she didn't try it alone.

Maybe Rafe was in Afghanistan working to save the hostages. She hadn't heard from him since he'd left. She'd give anything to hear his voice, even if he was yelling at her for taking chances with her life. It was hard to believe that they'd just met, and that he believed she was his soulmate. But she wasn't there yet, although she couldn't deny that there was a connection between them that she'd never experienced before. She prayed that she'd make it through this alive to see him again.

The car was slowing down, and Waltham slid the phone off his lap and returned it the hidden spot in the armrest. The vehicle she'd seen through the window was barreling toward them and kicking up enough dust to make it hard to see.

From the look of resignation on Waltham's face, she was almost certain they weren't going to be friendly.

"Remember what I said. Let me do the talking." Meghan nodded and took a deep breath to calm her heartbeat which threatened to jump out of her chest with every beat.

The armored truck caught up and herded them off the road. Waltham pulled to the side and stopped but he left the engine running. She'd love to know what he was thinking, but for the first time during the trip he was quiet. That would teach her to watch what she wished for.

Two men jumped out of the truck and approached the jeep. A third must have gotten out of the back since when she looked up there was a gun pointed at her head through her window. The other two approached Waltham, guns pointed directly at him. The one she assumed was in charge, motioned to him to open his window.

As he rolled it down, everything seemed to slow down. Her heart no longer beat in double or triple time. It was like the calm before the storm when everything is peaceful just before all hell breaks loose.

Unable to understand a word they were saying, she kept silent and still as Waltham instructed. The last thing she wanted was to look into the barrel of whatever type of gun was pointed at her face.

The man in black, Johnny Cash was probably

spinning in his grave, but she didn't know what else to call him, spoke in a language she couldn't understand. At first, Waltham answered in English, but then he switched to what had to be Pashto. No wonder Tex had sent him to help her. She was like a newborn babe out in the middle of nowhere and completely defenseless.

The only word she understood was 'no,' and Waltham was using it a lot. Probably not the best thing to yell at people who looked ready to kill. She didn't have to be a rocket scientist to know they weren't 'friendlies' and that these were the people she'd traveled to see.

The man in black yelled and the other two moved closer to the car. Waltham continued to argue and as his voice got angrier and Meghan hoped he wouldn't get them both shot. No sooner had the words formed in her mind when everything when to hell in a handbasket.

The leader yanked open the driver's door and dragged Waltham out of the jeep. Then he punched him in the stomach with his machine gun and knocked him to the ground.

As he struggled to get up, he glanced at her, motioning to stay put, and then pulled himself up. She wished she knew what they were saying, but even if she understood the language, they spoke so quickly she'd never have been able to keep up with them.

The one in charge was growing impatient. His

voice rose and he lifted his rifle. Meghan thought he was going to beat Waltham again, but instead, he pulled the trigger. She watched in disbelief as Waltham fell to the ground. It had to be a mistake, this couldn't be happening. Why They'd been driving to Bamyan and talking about tea and now his blood was spreading in the desert sand somewhere in the middle of Afghanistan.

She told herself to stay strong even though her stomach churned with fear and desperation. It wasn't looking good for, she was all alone in the middle of nowhere, with no way to defend herself. Her sole reason for being there was to talk to the Taliban, to hopefully get close to Charlie. Instead, she was miles and miles away from him and might never see him again. As she met the man in black's eyes, they opened her door and dragged her out of the jeep. Unsure what their next move would be, she braced for a bullet. It seemed the logical next step for them, so she was surprised and temporarily relieved when they pulled her toward their truck.

"Come."

"I have to get to Bamyan."

"You will come with us," his English was broken and stilted, but maybe he could understand her and let her go.

"No. I have to get to Bamyan. I am with the Press." He didn't look impressed. Or maybe he didn't understand. "Newspaper? I am writing a story."

"You come with us now." The man holding her arm raised his rifle.

"Can I get my pack?" At least then she might have a chance of contacting Tex as long as they didn't take her phone. Where her bravery came from, she had no clue, but she was going to go with it as long as possible.

After a moment, he nodded, and she went to the jeep and grabbed it from the floorboard. She didn't even have time to swing it onto her back before he dragged her away from the car and toward their armored truck.

She tried to see if Waltham was still alive but could only see his legs lying still in the sand. It was her fault this happened, she didn't even know if he had a family. If no one found his body, they would never know what happened and he'd be sucked into the desert and disappear forever.

"Come." She wondered if they knew any other English words. When she'd made the decision to try to save Charlie, she'd never considered they might not be able to communicate. Hopefully, she'd find someone that would be able to understand her.

After being shoved into the back of the truck, they used a zip tie on her hands and feet, then put a black bag type thing over her head. It smelled of blood and sweat and made her gag from the stench. Fear rose in her throat along with the bile as she thought about what had happened to the last person who'd worn it.

As the truck's engine roared to life, she prayed for Waltham, for Charlie, and for herself. It wasn't supposed to be like this. Rafe's words about leaving things to the professionals echoed in her brain and her heart ached knowing she'd probably never see him again. "I'm sorry, big guy. I do love you."

CHAPTER 15

It took almost an hour for Murph to free Miranda from the explosive laden belt. Not only were there several trip wires, but the seat itself was wired to explode if she stood up. They'd been worried about keeping Miranda calm, so she wouldn't accidentally trigger the explosives. Halo's presence helped at first, but once Cam flashed his big ole' blue eyes and bright white smile, she even smiled back. It was unexpected but whatever it took to keep her from freaking out was fine with them. The more still she remained the easier it was for Murph to work his magic. Leaving him and Cam inside, Rafe and Jake joined Ryan near the front of the cave to keep watch.

"Did you get new orders?" Rafe asked as they approached the cave opening.

"No. I haven't heard anything new."

"I wondered if that had just been for Miranda's benefit."

Jake tipped his head in agreement. "But I do know where the other hostages are. Mr. dirtbag finally spilled his guts. If he'd yelled much more, I'd have had to sic Halo on him."

"I'm surprised. I didn't think he'd give you anything. Hell, the way this operation was run, I didn't think he'd know anything," Ryan added as he joined their conversation.

"I agree. Considering she was their best chance at negotiation I don't understand why they had the "b team" in charge," Rafe added.

"Actually, he wasn't the "b team," Hibatullah was the brother of Azfaar, the local commander," Jake said as he pulled his map out of his pack.

"He's not going to be a happy camper when he finds out his brother is dead." Ryan smiled. He was the most bloodthirsty of the group when it came to the Taliban, but he had good reason for his hatred.

"So, what's the plan, boss?"

"If Miranda is okay to travel, we're going to rescue the other hostages."

"Where are they?" Rafe asked, and Jake put the map on the cave floor and pointed out their current location. "Hibatullah said they were in these mountains, about twenty klicks northwest."

"Do you think he was telling the truth?"

"I do. By then he was pleading for us to just take the girl and let him go. If we'd have been able to make EXFIL we'd have taken him with us. But I couldn't chance leaving him alive to alert his brother."

Rafe didn't want to think about his kills. There had been many over the last ten years for each of them, but they did what was necessary to carry out their mission. They would have gladly given their lives it if meant protecting their country. It made him think of Meghan. He wasn't even sure if she was back in DC at work or still in Atlanta. Either way, at least she was safe and hopefully soon her brother would be too.

"Did he say anything about additional men? Or supplies?"

"No. He went from screaming obscenities to pissing himself. But it wouldn't surprise me if there were more men coming."

"Did he have a standard check-in time?"

"He said no, but I took his phone, so we'll know as soon as his brother figures out we've got Miranda."

"Hopefully not until we're breathing down his neck. I'm still concerned he'll take out the rest of the hostages," Rafe said. He sure as hell didn't want to have that conversation with Meghan.

"He'd be pissed but he still reports to someone higher up the food chain. If he takes out their payday, he'll have to answer for it."

"True. Do we know who he reports to?"

"Hibatullah said he didn't know."

"Copy that."

"We're good, boss," Murph announced as he approached them followed closely by Cam, Halo, and Miranda. She was holding her side as she limped along. Her face looked like hell.

"Good. How is she?"

"She's got a couple of broken ribs, a bruised knee, and we need to follow concussion protocol, they did a number on her head and face."

"Can she walk?"

"I can. I won't hold you up. I just want to get out of here. Please don't leave me."

"Darlin, we'd never leave you," Cam said before Jake had a chance to respond. Rafe and Murph exchanged looks and Murph shrugged his shoulders. There was a story there and he'd get it out of Murph later.

"We don't leave anyone behind, Miranda. You'll be safe with us. But you need to let us know if you're hurting. We have medical supplies and we can give you something for the pain."

"Thank you. But I want to have my wits about me. There were others and I know they're coming back. I don't want to be here."

"You won't. We'll be leaving shortly. Ryan, check her out, see if you can do anything to make her more comfortable."

"Sure thing." As Ryan led her over to one of the chairs used by the guards, Jake turned to the others.

"I'm checking in with TOC to give them the update on Miranda. Hopefully, they have more intel, but if not, we've got a twenty click hike to the location of the other hostages based on what Hibatullah told me. If she can't walk, we'll take turns carrying her."

"Copy that."

"TOC may not like it, but we're stuck waiting to be extracted until nightfall. Might as well make use of our time."

It was the same decision he'd have made if he was in charge and Rafe was relieved. Even if he didn't have a connection to one of the hostages, they were Americans and they couldn't leave them behind. It would have gone against everything he believed in.

Jake moved away to contact command while the rest of the team watched Ryan perform a triage assessment on Miranda. Rafe winced when Ryan lifted her pant leg and exposed the black and purple lump that had been her knee and shin.

"What the fuck did they do to her?" Cam muttered low enough so she wouldn't hear him.

"They wanted to make sure she couldn't make a run for it if she managed to get away. It's SOP in situations like this," Murph answered. "She must have given them a hard time, or I doubt they would have roughed her up since they were using her for a trade."

"There's no way she's walking on that leg." Rafe

wasn't sure how she'd managed to walk out of the cave on it.

"Agreed," Jake said. "We'll take turns carrying her. I figure we have a couple of hours before Azfaar will call his brother. When I checked his phone, Hibatullah had a call just before we breached. We may have gotten lucky."

"What did TOC say?"

"Nothing we don't already know. They are sending the drone to the location Hibatullah gave us to see if they can get confirmation that the hostages are there."

"The captain isn't thrilled. I don't think he believes we couldn't make the EXFIL."

"I guess we should have sent pictures of her wired up to the chair," Murph groused. "It was a bitch to disarm. Whoever rigged that sucker didn't intend for her to get out of it."

"They were going to get confirmation of the hostage release and then just leave her there?" Cam asked.

"Most likely. It's not like we haven't seen it before. That's why we don't do deals. You're still new, wait a few more years."

"There is one other thing," Jake said as he met Rafe's eyes. "There has been an escalation of Taliban activity near Bamyan. They shot an employee of the British Embassy, but he was found alive—barely—by a patrol. He told them that he was traveling with a woman. An American journalist. They took her."

If his heart could have stopped at that moment, it would have. He didn't need Jake to confirm it, he knew with his whole being that the journalist was Meghan.

"Do we know where they've taken her?"

"No, but if I had to guess we'll find her with the other hostages. Tex got a message to TOC that she was heading there to interview Azfaar and hopefully secure their release. He also had a message for you, said to tell you he was sorry. Your woman has a set of balls on her. I'll give her that."

A deep bone-chilling cold spread through Rafe's chest. Cast iron balls or not, after he rescued her, he was going to kill her for putting herself in danger.

"Who are we talking about?" Murph asked.

"Rafe's woman. The one he met in the airport," Ryan responded.

"What was she thinking?"

"She wasn't, not clearly at least. She wanted to rescue her brother," Rafe replied. "He's one of the other hostages."

"Do you mean Charlie's sister, Meghan, came here?" Miranda asked.

"Yes. Meghan Henley."

"I met her once before we left. She's amazing."

"Yes, she is," Rafe said through gritted teeth.

"Tex also said that her tracking device is still active."

"What tracking device?"

"The one he put in the phone he sent to Meghan to bring on her trip. He said the signal was moving toward the location we got for the other hostages."

"I may have to fly up there and kiss that man when we get back. Then I'm going to kick his ass for putting my woman in danger."

Jake actually laughed. "From what he said, and what you've told me, I don't think either of you stood a chance against her."

This time Rafe smiled though he was sure it looked more like a grimace.

"Are we going now? I'm ready," Miranda said, and they all turned to look at her. She was quite a woman. After all, she'd been through, she was ready to go help rescue her friends. Most of the women he'd met would have been crying and begging to go home.

"Yes, ma'am," Jake answered as he scooped her into his arms. "But you get to ride."

"I can walk."

"Sure, you can, but we can move a lot faster this way. We have a lot of terrain to cover."

"Won't I slow you down having to carry me? It's not like I'm a sack of potatoes."

"You won't. We train for this all the time. Just hold on and let me know if you're in pain."

Miranda nodded but didn't say anything.

"Cam, you and Halo take point."

"Copy that."

Silently they moved across the hills keeping to the shadows and brush hoping to avoid detection. It would have been faster without Miranda, but no one complained. They switched who was carrying her every half hour. Ryan gave her an injection for the pain and thankfully, she slept through most of it. With her broken ribs and being carried and moving at the pace they were, it would have been extremely painful.

It had been just over two hours since they'd set out for their new location when Jake gave them the signal to stop. They crouched in place and waited. Rafe could see his lips moving but he was speaking so low he couldn't make out what he was saying. Then his voice whispered in his ear.

"I just got an update from TOC. We have confirmation of the hostages' location. They're in a compound about five klicks from here."

"Did they say anything about Meghan?"

"No, but we're going on the assumption that she will be with the other hostages."

"Copy that."

"When we get within range of the compound, we'll do some recon and come up with our plan."

"Okay, boss." Rafe hated not having confirmation of Meghan's location, but Jake was right. It made sense that they'd bring her to the same location as the other hostages. He prayed they hadn't hurt her or worse. The Taliban were irrational fanatics and trying to anticipate their next move was like playing whack-a-mole.

Love at first sight had been a joke to him, something they wrote about in books. How could anyone really fall for someone right away? Lust yes, but love? He'd never have believed it possible until his eyes met hers in that airport. It was like lightning struck and even then, he hadn't believed it. Not until he held her on the plane. From that moment on he knew he'd never let her go. Since then her beautiful face and full lips have haunted his dreams. He ached to hold her, to make love to her, to wrap her up and keep her safe for the rest of their lives. God help anyone who hurt a hair on her head.

BY THE TIME they were within range, it was just after noon and the sun was high in the sky. As they made their way through the hills toward the compound, they'd had to stop when Miranda woke. Rafe had been carrying her, when she got restless. He checked her pulse and discovered she was burning up with fever. Ryan gave her a shot of antibiotics and cleaned her wounds. They had no choice but to continue on and pray that she'd survive until they could get her medical attention at the base.

Cam had been the only one who hadn't taken a turn carrying her since he'd been on point with Halo. Now that they were within striking distance of the compound, he held on to her like he'd never let her go. Rafe recognized the look on Cam's face even if the kid didn't realize it yet. Miranda was going to have a lot to deal with when she got back home, and he hoped that Cam would be able to give her the time she needed to heal.

Jake updated command on their current location and Miranda's condition. Then he got the latest intel from the drone reconnaissance. At this point, they had no idea how many tangos were waiting for them or where they were holding the hostages. They'd go in blind if they had to, but Rafe was really hoping they'd have something for Jake.

"Do you want the good news or bad news first," Jake asked.

"Good."

"We think we know where they're holding the hostages, and from the heat signatures it looks like Meghan is with them." Relief poured over Rafe like a waterfall, but it was only temporary.

"And the bad news," Murph asked.

"They are on the second floor with only one way in or out and it's heavily guarded. TOC said there are at least fifty tangos at the compound."

"Well fuck me running," Ryan said with a sigh. "What's the plan?"

"For you? You're staying with Miranda. You'll be able to keep her stable."

Rafe knew Ryan was disappointed. He practically drooled at any opportunity to kill members of the Taliban. But he was also the most qualified to treat Miranda.

"Okay, Boss."

"We're going to get some help with air cover. The plan is to deliver a few presents to our friends. It should draw them away from the hostages so we can move in and grab them."

"It could work," Rafe acknowledged. "Getting in is one thing. What's our plan to get them out of there?"

"That's where the bad news comes in."

"You mean the fifty tangos wasn't the bad news?" Cam asked.

"No. The bad news is we don't know the condition of any of the hostages and we have to get them here," Jake pointed to a spot on the map. "That's where they'll have the chopper waiting for us."

Rafe studied the map, it had to be at least two klicks from the compound. If more than a few of them were injured it was going to be a clusterfuck.

"They can't get in any closer?"

"Too dangerous."

"What if we blow up the whole compound once we're clear. Then they could land here," Rafe said as he pointed to a spot about eight hundred feet from the compound's walls.

"That could work. Let me talk to the captain. In the meantime, you and Murph find the best entry point."

"Okay." Anything was better than sitting and waiting. Knowing Meghan was just out of reach and possibly hurt was a distraction, one he couldn't afford with so many lives on the line.

The brush was sparse, making it difficult to stay out of sight as they scoped out their options. There were only two entry points, the main gate with four guards or the rear gate. The rear entrance would be the better option, but it was further from the main building where the hostages were located. The Taliban soldiers might run when the bombing started, or they might stand their ground which would make it impossible for them to get in without being seen. They'd need a plan B and probably plan C if things went as usual.

"What are you thinking," Murph asked.

"I'm thinking we need to set some remote detonations in the compound in case they don't run when the bombing starts."

"Near the rear guard shack and the outbuilding on the left?"

"Exactly."

Before Rafe could hit his com, Jake's voice whispered in their ears. It was as if Jake read their minds, but then he knew them as well as they knew themselves.

"Eagle 2, sitrep."

"Rear entry is the best option. But we'll need a distraction if the bombing doesn't draw out the tangos. We want to set some remote devices."

"Copy that. Get back here and we'll discuss."

"We can do it while we're here."

"It's too soon. We're not ready if you get spotted."

"Copy that, Eagle 2 out."

Rafe took one more look through his field glasses to see if he could locate any of the hostages but there was no sign of them.

CHAPTER 16

Thirsty, hot, and nauseated from the smell of blood and sweat from the hood they'd put over her head, Meghan wished she could take back every mean thought she'd had while traveling with Waltham.

The men in the back of the truck laughed and poked her occasionally as they chatted back and forth like they were on some kind of a joy ride. No one had said a word to her after they'd shoved her into the back of the armored truck. Did she wish she'd listened to Rafe? Hell yeah. But she knew that if she'd waited for the state department to do anything, they'd probably never see Charlie alive. Did it stop her from being terrified that they were going to shoot her or worse? Nope.

There should be some kind of kidnapping one-oh-one class. Her self-defense classes taught her how to handle herself in case she was grabbed on the street, but nothing prepared her for this. Somehow, she doubted that trying to make them see her as human would help since they had such a low opinion of women.

They hit a large bump in the road, and she got knocked into the side of the truck. It reminded her how badly she had to pee. While she argued back and forth with herself about trying to talk to the men, the vehicle slowed and then stopped. The clank and squeal of the metal door opening sent a shiver of fear down her spine. Huddling against the cold metal side of the truck, she curled into herself as much as possible hoping they'd forget about her. The dark made everything more intense and her heart beat so fast it sounded like drums pounding in her ears. She needed to calm down. To listen and figure out her surroundings if she wanted to get out of there alive. Forcing herself to focus, she took slow, deep breaths.

"Come." Meghan wondered once again if they knew any other words in English. One of the men grabbed her arm and pulled her out of the truck and let her fall to the ground. Trying to stand with her wrists and ankles still zip tied was difficult. It must have been taking her too long because he yanked her arm and pulled her to her feet. It took everything she had not to burst into tears. There was more shouting, and the hood was pulled from her head. She took huge gulps of fresh air and her nausea subsided. Then the ties on her wrists and ankles were cut off sending shooting pains up her arms and legs as the blood flow returned.

"Open your eyes," a heavily accented voice commanded. Meghan slowly lifted her eyelids, but it was too bright after the hours under the dark hood. It took a few times before she was able to keep them open in the light.

"You wanted to write story. Yes?"

Meghan turned toward the voice while trying to memorize her surroundings. "Yes. But I was supposed to go to Bamyan."

"You don't need there. The story is here."

"Where is here? I'm supposed to meet with Azfaar."

"Yes. You will. Soon. Now come with me." At least he wasn't dragging her like the others had, she followed him through a courtyard area with flowers and trees and children running around. Then he led her into the largest of the buildings.

"I need to go to the bathroom." She'd been holding it for hours and she wasn't sure how much longer she could wait. He'd been nicer than the others, she took a chance that he'd understand and take pity on her.

"You need to wait."

"I don't think I can. I've waited a long time." He didn't say anything at first but led her down a different hallway and stopped in front of a door.

"You go." After a moment's hesitation about what she'd find on the other side of the door,

Meghan reached for the doorknob with trepidation.

"Go, now."

"Okay." Taking a deep breath, she turned the knob and pushed open the door. The room was dark, and it took a moment for her eyes to adjust. The only light was a small lantern burning near the sink. Letting out the breath she'd been holding, she made a beeline for the toilet.

As she washed her hands and splashed water on her face, she saw her reflection in the mirror and barely recognized herself. Her black hair was tangled and knotted and even dragging her fingers through it didn't fix it. The bags and shadows were so dark under her eyes she looked like one of the walking dead.

A sharp knock on the door made her jump and sent her heart racing. "Hurry up." The voice was different, not the same heavy accent as before. Praying that she'd at least see her brother before they killed her, she pulled open the door and stepped out to face the muzzle of a gun.

"Enough stalling. Come with us." They didn't give her much choice. One of the other men grabbed her arm and dragged her down the hall. The man who'd let her use the bathroom was nowhere to be seen. Maybe he'd gotten into trouble for showing her kindness.

The hallway was plain, mostly bare walls and lots of doors. As she was pulled along, she continued to catalog everything she saw, hoping it would come back to her if she had the opportunity to escape. They climbed a flight of stairs and then walked down a hall lined with heavy metal doors. At the tenth door, they stopped. Fear sent shivers down her spine. This wasn't the type of door to keep people out, it was meant to keep someone in. Up until then, she'd still hoped they were taking her to Azfaar for the pre-arranged interview.

The first guard tapped keys on the electronic pad and the door clicked open. Without a word, they shoved her inside and slammed it shut behind her. The echo of the door clicking shut was so final that she was resigned to the thought that she'd never leave the cell or see her brother again. A noise made her turn around and she realized she wasn't alone. They'd put her in with the other hostages.

"Charlie!" He was there, standing less than two feet away. Had she really found him? Racing to him, she hugged him tightly, relief at having found him bringing tears to her eyes. She didn't let go, wouldn't let go, she was too afraid he might disappear. That none of this was real.

"Meghan? What on earth are you doing here?"

"Oh my God, Charlie. I never thought I'd see you again."

"Meggy..." He held her as tightly as she was holding him. Like they were hanging on for dear life. "But I don't understand why you're here. Why would you put yourself in danger?"

"You're my brother. What else would I do?" Then she looked around the cell at all the other faces, haggard, dirty, but with a bit of hope in their eyes probably for the first time since they'd been taken.

"Listen. They don't know I'm related to Charlie. We have to keep it that way."

"Why would it matter?"

"Because they'd use us against each other. No matter what, if anything happens. I'm just another hostage. Don't interfere, any of you. Our lives could depend on that. Okay?" She watched as they all nodded their heads.

"I get the feeling there is more than you're telling us."

"Don't worry. Everything will be okay. Hey, where's Miranda?" Meghan hoped she sounded convincing. The last thing she wanted was to make it worse for them. They'd been through enough already.

"They took her the second day we were here after they found out she was a senator's daughter."

"Fuck."

"Meghan," Charlie exclaimed.

"Really, Charlie? You're a captive of the Taliban and you're worried about me saying fuck?"

"Yes, because our faith is all we have right now." Meghan sighed.

"How did you get here? Are there others coming for us? Will help be coming soon?" The rest of the hostages finally realized she was really there, and the questions came too quickly for her to answer.

"How I got here is a story for another time. The government knows you're here. They will come as soon as they can." Praying that she was right and that a rescue was already in work, she tried to sound more positive than she felt.

"Are any of you hurt?"

"No, we're fine."

"Meggy, I still can't believe you're really here."

"Truthfully? Me either. Remember, no matter what they do or say, you don't know me. Right?"

"Right, I promise. Do you know why they're keeping us here?"

"My friend thinks they are trying to ransom you for weapons. It's probably why they haven't hurt you."

"Or God's been protecting us." Meghan wasn't sure about that, but if his faith was that strong maybe it was true. Who was she to doubt anything at that point?

The cell didn't have much space. A few filthy mattresses were strewn around the cement floor, a bucket, and a small window blocked by heavy bars.

"I'm so glad you're okay," she said and then wobbled on her feet.

"Sit down, you look like you're going to fall over."

He was right, she was at the end of her rope. The relief at finding Charlie and the others alive sucked all of her energy, and everything she'd gone through in the last twenty-four hours flooded back. Sliding to the floor, she pulled up her knees and wrapped her arms around them. Exhausted and emotionally raw, she leaned on her brother's shoulder and closed her eyes for a few moments.

The sound of a cell door slamming woke her. "Oh God. I didn't mean to fall asleep."

"Meggy, please. You've been through hell. You needed it. You weren't out for long."

Searching for her pack to grab a bottle of water, she remembered they took it off of her back when they'd tied her hands and feet in the truck. It was probably still in there unless they'd found it. If they searched the bag, they'd find her press credentials and the phone. Once they realized who she was she'd probably be the next news story.

"Why would you risk yourself?"

"You're my brother. Are you kidding me? I had to do something. I arranged an interview with the local leader. I thought the press coverage might make him want to release you."

"Did you see him?"

"No. They shot my driver and took me before I could get to Bamyan to meet him. I thought maybe I'd get to see him still, I doubt that'll happen now."

The more she thought about it, the more stupid she felt. If they were going to let her interview

Azfaar, she would have been taken to him right away instead of being locked up. Chances are they never planned on letting her get near him. When she and Tex had gone over all the possible scenarios, getting captured and killed had been one of them. He made sure she understood the real risks with her decision to go forward. She hadn't cared, she had to try to save her brother since the government wasn't doing jack.

If Rafe's team had been sent to rescue the missionaries, then Tex would have tried harder to talk her out of going. That much she'd figured out on her own. She would never regret trying to help Charlie and the others even if she failed. And if by some miracle they got out of this, she'd have one hell of a story to tell.

There had to be something she could do. Some move she could make. What was the worse that would happen? They'd kill her? That was a distinct possibility anyway. She hadn't come this far to just give up no matter how scared she felt on the inside. With her mind made up, she got off the floor and pounded on the door.

"What are you doing?"

"Trying to get them to give me my backpack."

"Are you crazy?" one of the other missionaries asked. "You're going to bring them in here. You don't know what will happen."

"No, I don't, but I have to try to get us out of here."

189

"You're going to get us killed."

"Be quiet, if she wants to try, I say let her," Charlie said.

At first, there was no response, and she wondered if they might not leave any guards. It's not like they could break out, there wasn't even a keypad inside the cell, they might as well be in a cement box with a metal lid. She was about to give up when a small window opened in the door. She hadn't noticed that before.

"You can pound all you want. It will change nothing." Maybe not, but she got a response and that was something.

"I want my pack. I had it when I was brought here."

"You are in no place to make demands. You should be happy you're still breathing." The guard's accent was British and something else which made him easier to understand than any of the others.

"I am a journalist. I came from America to meet with Azfaar. To tell his story to the world." If they didn't know who she was they would as soon as they went through her pack. She didn't think it would matter if they had more information.

"Azfaar doesn't deal with women," the man said and slid the metal plate closed.

The guard may not have realized it, but he gave Meghan a lot of information. Azfaar was the local Taliban leader in Bamyan, that the guard knew who he was meant she was in his territory.

"Well that did you a lot of good, didn't it?"

"You know, if you don't stuff it, I may have to come over there and kick you." The guy was on her last nerve. Instead of being happy to see someone who was there to help he was being a pain in the ass.

"Meggy, please. Everyone is on edge."

"I'm not the one starting it." Yeah, she was being ornery but dammit the guy could be a little nicer, he was a missionary. Where was his brotherly love?

"I'm so glad I found you," she said as she held onto Charlie's hand, afraid to let him go now that she'd found him.

"I am too. I just hate that you put yourself in danger like this."

"I told Lizzie I'd find you. We kept it from Mom. Trying to explain it would have been hard. She's gotten a lot worse over the past couple of months."

"I'm sorry I put the family through all of this. But it's my calling. I'd do it again even knowing the consequences."

"I know. But can you go to someplace a little safer next time?"

Charlie chuckled. "Let's get out of this mess first. Okay?"

"Amen to that. I wonder what is going to happen next. Do they have a schedule where they feed you or anything?"

"Not really. It's like when they remember they give us some bottles of water and some bread."

"I guess we just wait and see."

About an hour later they found out what was coming next. Hearing the beep of the numbers on the keypad, Meghan moved to the other side of the cell putting as much distance as she could from Charlie. As the door opened, they all tensed. Meghan wished she had something to use as a weapon so she could try to break them out of there, but there was nothing.

"You, come with us."

"Why, where are you taking me?"

"No questions. Come." This guy sounded like one of the guys in the desert. What was it with these asshats? Then Tex's voice echoed in her head. "Women have no worth there, except for cooking, keeping house and making babies. You need to remember that."

Meghan looked over at Charlie as one of the gun-toting guards stepped into the cell to grab her. She silently pleaded that he wouldn't do anything to stop them from taking her, there was no doubt in her mind that they'd use that information against them.

After they dragged her from the cell, she prayed that they were taking her to see Azfaar after all.

The guards surrounded her, one in front and two behind. The two in back had their guns trained on her, leaving her no hope in hell that she'd be able to get away. It was ironic since they believed that women were nothing, yet they needed three guards for her. Maybe they were told that American women were more dangerous.

The dungeon looking area was left behind, and the stark cement walls and floors changed to murals, oriental carpets and antique furniture. It was like they were in two different buildings. It gave her hope that they were bringing her to Azfaar. Taking her all this way just to kill her seemed kind of crazy, but then she was dealing with the Taliban.

All the guards Meghan had seen were dressed alike in black with most of their faces covered. It made it impossible to tell who they were. She'd lost her head scarf in the desert and was surprised they hadn't given her something to cover her head. Or maybe it wouldn't matter because they planned to remove it from her shoulders soon.

While following the guard through the various corridors, she tried to come up with what she would say to Azfaar. How to reason with him, and hopefully get him to release the captives. It was a long shot, but she'd come too far not to try at least.

The guard in front of her stopped and opened another door. At least it wasn't metal, but her heart sank when she followed him into the room. It was some sort of a recording studio. A single chair was in the center of the room against a gray cement wall similar to the cell she'd just left. A video camera set up on a tripod and an easel were across from the chair.

"Sit," Guard number one said. Then he pointed to a poster balanced on the easel. "You will read this, exactly as written, or we will shoot you."

Meghan cringed as she looked at what they wanted her to read.

"Say the words."

"I won't. Go ahead and shoot me."

"Azfaar expected that response. If you don't cooperate, we will shoot her." A young girl, maybe ten, stood next to guard number two. He had his gun held against the child's head. What was wrong with these people?

"Please, don't hurt her." She had been a fool to think she could outsmart or even reason with them. They were ruthless and she was an infidel as far as they were concerned.

"Then read. Make it convincing." Guard number three moved from the doorway to the tripod and repositioned the camera until it was focused on her position, then started the recording. "Say the words or she will die."

The words were traitorous and untrue, but if she didn't do as they asked an innocent child would die, and it would be her fault. This was not one of the scenarios Tex had discussed. The Taliban usually just demanded ransoms, or they'd sell the captives for arms. This was more of an ISIS tactic.

"You're trying my patience. Say the words." The girl had tears running down her cheeks, but she didn't make a sound. God knows what they'd already put her through.

"Let her go and I will do it. But I want you to promise she won't be hurt."

"You have no say here. Read it or she dies." She'd exhausted all the options she'd been able to come up with and had no choice but to give in to their demands. They slid the easel a bit closer to the camera, which would ensure they captured her full face and would make it look like she was just speaking and not reading their prompts. Sighing, Meghan looked at the camera and read what was written on the poster board. The hate laden words sickened her.

"I am a non-believer and one of the foreign occupiers. Americans are greedy infidels who want to take over the world. You have no right to be here and no right to take our people prisoner. You will release the ten prisoners taken yesterday or they will kill me. You have three days to comply."

Meghan didn't know how she got through it. But they weren't happy with her performance. After her first attempt, the second guard who'd been holding the gun on the child, punched her in the face hard enough to knock her out of the chair. Her eye swelled up almost immediately. While she was on the ground, he kicked her over and over until the one in charge told him to stop.

"Do it again."

It was hard to read the words with her eye swollen and the pain radiating from her ribs. She got through it again, but they still weren't satisfied. The only saving grace for Meghan was that the little girl was gone, and she prayed that they had let her go.

She lost track of how many times she repeated the words or how many beatings she endured. By the time they were done, the room was spinning, she was nauseated from the blood in her mouth, and was unable to see clearly. Excruciating pain racked her body with every breath. Tears slid down her cheeks, but she no longer cared. All she wanted was for the pain to stop.

As her captors argued, probably about how to kill her, she prayed for a bullet in the head. Something fast, that would end the pain. One of them approached her but her vision was too blurred to know if it was the one who'd been beating her. Bracing herself for whatever was coming next, she was surprised when he grabbed her wrists and tied them to the chair behind her, then tied her ankles to the legs. It was kind of comical that they actually believed she could walk let alone try to escape.

She must have passed out at some point. Blinking a few times, she attempted to clear her vision. It was blurry but she could make out enough of her surroundings to know she was alone. The rumbling sound of an explosion rocked the building. Then it happened again, this time closer and ten times louder. The floor shook and dust filled the air making it harder for her to breathe.

It had to be Rafe and his team. Joy filled her heart that he'd come to save her, to save them all. Her pain addled mind never took into account that he wouldn't expect her to be in Afghanistan or to even look for her. Instead, she struggled with her bindings, trying to release her hands but all she did was make them bleed.

Then a third bomb exploded, and part of the ceiling came down, hitting her. As she lost consciousness, she prayed, "Please God, I need to tell Rafe I love him."

CHAPTER 17

The team reviewed the plan and tweaked it once Rafe and Murph returned from their exploration of the compound. It was just a matter of waiting for the bombers to be in range. Expecting to get the go order, instead Jake received a secure call from Captain Knox. That usually meant something went sideways. It happened more often than not, and they were used to it. But this time it was different for Rafe. This time the woman he loved was suffering through who knows what and he needed to save her.

For the last hour, he couldn't shake the feeling that Meghan was in extreme danger. It ate away at his self-discipline and chiseled away at his focus. Only his years of training kept him from storming the walls and rescuing his woman. Instead, he remained alert and ready to move as soon as they were given the go order. He had no choice, he'd be no good to her or his team if he ran off half-cocked.

While Jake was talking to the captain, the team went over the plan one more time looking for any holes they could fill. It was about as tight as they could make it without knowing how the tangos would respond once the bombs started falling. The drones used thermal imaging on each pass overhead to give them the location of everyone in the compound. There was a cluster of people in the right wing of the main building. From the schematics TOC sent, it had double walls and then a central location of inner cells and that was their destination. Rafe just prayed that they had Meghan with the other captives.

"TOC confirmed that Meghan was brought to the compound. Our latest scans show there are still only the nine hostages together in the one cell. So, she's there but not being held with the others as of the last scan of the location."

"Do they have confirmation of her death?" Rafe asked through gritted teeth and a tight jaw.

"No."

"Then she's alive in there somewhere and I intend to find her with or without permission."

Before Jake could answer the other's voiced their agreement. "I already told the captain the same thing. No worries, Rafe. We will find Meghan and extract her with the other hostages."

Rafe nodded, relieved that he wouldn't have to go against orders to save his woman. "Do we have any idea where she is?"

Jake averted his eyes, and the momentary relief he'd felt evaporated. "We know where she was a short time ago. There is a video circulating on the internet. She's the only captive visible and was savagely beaten."

Groaning inside, it made him more resigned than ever to get in there and take out everyone he came across.

"Beaten but not executed. Correct?" Ryan asked the words Rafe couldn't bring himself to utter.

Jake nodded. "No, not executed. She was alive when the recording cut off."

"When do we breach?"

"We go in with the initial bomb drop which should happen in the next few minutes. I know you're more than ready to finish this but remember, we don't know the condition of any of the captives, this may be a huge clusterfuck," Jake said as he checked his pack.

"Copy that."

"Ryan, watch for stragglers. TOC has the medical team at Bagram on alert for Miranda. Keep her alive until we can get her there. Once the bombs stop, make your way to the EXFIL point with Miranda and we'll rendezvous there with the other hostages."

"Copy that, Boss." He tilted his chin in Rafe's direction. It was all they needed to say to each other, and Rafe repeated the action.

As they set off, Rafe murmured under his breath, "Spitfire, just hold on a little longer. I'm coming, sweetheart."

THE FIRST BOMB dropped as they made it to the rear entrance. Rafe and Murph went over the wall and set the secondary explosives. They finished as the second bomb rocked the compound. From their location, they observed the chaos that ensued. Not all of the Taliban soldiers were well-trained, most were conscripts taken from the surrounding villages and hamlets and barely old enough to shave. But it didn't mean they weren't dangerous.

The third bomb exploded, and they blew their charges and took off toward the main building. Halo led the way and would warn them about any tangos still lurking. Just past the rear guard shack, Rafe and Halo saw movement at the same time. Halo attacked with Rafe at his heels. Two men were hiding, but when Halo pounced on one of them, the other screamed and threw down his gun. They were quickly secured with zip ties and the SEALs moved on to their primary objective.

It wouldn't take long for the Taliban to return

once the bombing stopped. The hostages were too valuable to abandon. But if he stayed true to form, Azfaar would be long gone and leave his peons to bring the captives to a new location and clean up the mess. The only variable was if he'd found out they already rescued the senator's daughter, then it could go either way. There was still the chance that he could have discovered that his brother, Hibatullah, had been taken out, and he might decide to cut his losses.

The bombing worked as they'd hoped, and most of the soldiers had been taken out by the explosions or deserted their posts. They met with little resistance until they entered the second floor wing where they expected to find the hostages. Halo alerted them to the Taliban soldiers who'd stayed behind.

Jake's voice whispered in their ears. "We're looking at ten tangos. Eagle 5 go in low. Eagle 2 will follow. The stability of the building is questionable. No explosives until we get the hostages out."

"Copy that."

"Eagle 4 and I will be watching your six."

Rafe tapped Cam on the shoulder signaling he was ready, and they moved toward the doorway. Machine gun fire riddled the walls around them. Once they made it through the doorway Rafe picked off two, and Cam and Halo took out a third.

"Three tangos down," Rafe reported, as they turned the corner. The hallway was dark, no lights, no windows. Signaling to Cam to put on their night vision devices.

"Eagle 1, NVDs needed."

"Copy that, Eagle 2." The night vision gave them an edge as they continued down the corridor. Halo took out another tango before Rafe and Cam even saw him. The soldier's shriek as the dog attacked alerted the others to their presence but not where they were. Rafe took out number four with a quick slice through his carotid artery. More gunfire echoed behind them, but Jake and Murph had that handled.

Continuing down the hall they came across the first of the cells. The door was open and empty. Rafe sure as hell hoped their intel wasn't FUBAR and that the hostages hadn't been moved before the breach. There was always the chance there were tunnels under the building, and they'd gotten them out of there.

The second cell door was closed, and they couldn't tell from looking through the small door if there was anyone in there injured and not able to respond.

"We need to blow this door. Unless you can figure out the code?"

Jake responded, "Copy that. Murph, go ahead. Blow the door but keep it small we don't want the building coming down on our heads."

Murph and Jake had caught up to them as they'd cleared the open cell. They needed to get the fuck out of there and make it to the EXFIL point. Time was getting sparse and they hadn't found any of the hostages.

After Murph set the charge, they stood back while it blew then checked only to find another empty cell. "Fuck. Are we sure they didn't move them after the last drone check?" Murph asked.

"They're here, but it could be any one of these cells. Keep looking." There were two other open cells, then they came to another locked door. Except this time when they peeked through the opening, they found the hostages.

"Back away from the door," Murph yelled and Rafe watched to make sure they moved as far as possible.

"Blow it."

They got the door open and all nine of the remaining missionary group was there but not Meghan. His heart twisted. He'd prayed they'd have put her with the others but maybe they hadn't had a chance to figure out her connection to the group.

"We're here to rescue you. Anyone injured? Unable to walk?" They looked rough, dirty and tired, but mostly unharmed.

"No, we're okay. All of us can walk. But where's my sister? Did you find Meghan?" It had to be Charlie.

"Not yet. But she was here with you, right?"

"She was but they took her away a few hours ago and didn't bring her back. You have to find her. I'm not leaving without her."

"Is everyone else accounted for?" Jake asked, cutting off Charlie.

"Miranda is gone too. They took her a few days ago."

"We have her. She's okay."

"We'll find her, Charlie, I promise," Rafe said. The man looked inconsolable and they needed to get them out of there so he could find Meghan.

"Rafe, enough, we need to move. Now," Jake interjected. "Cam take point, we'll pull up the rear. Keep your eyes open."

"We're going to get you out of here. Follow behind him and keep going no matter what." A couple of the women were crying, but they listened and lined up behind Cam to follow him to safety.

"Rafe, take Murph and find Meghan. I'll go with Cam. Once we've got them to the EXFIL we'll be back."

"Copy that."

"You'll find her."

"I know," Rafe gave his friend and boss a grim smile. He'd find her, he just prayed she'd still be alive when he did.

After checking the remaining cells, they still hadn't found Meghan. What the fuck had they done with her?

"Eagle 1, all cells checked no sign of the HVT."

"Hold on." Rafe heard him asking the hostages if they'd been held anywhere else in the compound.

"No, they kept us in the cell except when they were making the videos. Then we were on the other side of the building."

"Did you hear that? Go back to the main hallway, then turn left. It's the living area."

"Copy that." Rafe took off down the hallway and Murph followed. They were running out of time but there wasn't a snowball's chance in hell he was leaving without Meghan.

The living quarters had been the part of the building that had taken the biggest hit from the bombs. As they made their way through the rubble, they came across a few bodies, but none of them were Meghan. They cleared room after room and Rafe's despair was growing by the moment.

"Rafe, I found her," Murph called to him from the recording studio. There had been some damage, but the room wasn't toast like some of the others.

"Meghan," Rafe asked gently as he touched her swollen face and checked for a pulse. She was alive, thank God, but her pulse was weak. She looked nothing like the woman who'd kissed him goodbye in the Atlanta airport. Just seeing her like this filled him with rage and he wanted to kill everyone all over again.

"Let's get her untied. Ryan will work on her when we get to the helo. It might be a blessing if she doesn't wake up until we get there," Murph said and sliced through the ropes tying her hands at the back of the chair. Rafe cursed himself for losing focus, and silently sliced through the ropes at her feet. When he picked her up it was like lifting a doll, she was so tiny and limp.

"Go, I'm going to grab what I can find and be right behind you."

"Copy that."

Rafe moved with speed and precision through the destroyed building, working his way over broken furniture and pieces of concrete. He hadn't expected to find anyone else alive, so when he came face-to-face with a Taliban soldier with a machine gun, he cursed. He'd never let his guard down before.

But Murph had his six, and a single shot flew past his ear. The Taliban soldier hit the ground with a bullet in the center of his forehead.

"Rafe, I know what you're thinking and you're wrong. You have a wounded civilian in your arms, your mission is to rescue her. Now stop thinking so much and let's get the fuck out of here."

Rafe nodded. "I owe you."

"You don't owe me a fucking thing. We're brothers."

"Eagle 2, sitrep."

"Eagle 1, we're on the way out with the last captive."

"Copy that. Now get your asses to the EXFIL."

The chopper was waiting at the evac point. Everyone was loaded and waiting for them to return. Rafe had the unconscious Meghan in his arms as they ran for the chopper. Murph took out the few tangos who were still hoping for a piece of them.

As the helo took off, the SEALs exchanged glances. This had been one hell of a clusterfuck, but they'd gotten everyone out alive. It was a win-win as far as they were concerned. There had been too many missions that hadn't gone this well even with all the complications. They probably wouldn't know how to react if they went in and got out as planned.

"How's Miranda?" Jake asked over their coms.

"Stable for now. Not sure if there's something internal going on though," Ryan answered. He was kneeling between his two patients. Meghan still hadn't regained consciousness.

"And Meghan?" Rafe asked.

"Not sure, bro. From the look of this head wound, she's definitely got a concussion. It's not good we can't wake her up," Ryan said. "I'm sorry, Rafe. But I just don't know. The medical team at Bagram will have a better idea."

Rafe nodded. His face set in stone as usual, but inside his heart was breaking for his little spitfire.

She had to come back to him. The universe couldn't be so cruel to let him find her and then lose her.

"Let me by, I want to see my sister," Charlie Henley said as he pushed his way past the others in his group to get to Meghan.

"Hold up there," Jake said, "she's unconscious. You need to let the medic do his job."

"I won't interfere, but I need to see her."

Jake nodded, and let him pass. They were about a half hour out of Bagram and they didn't want to have to sedate anyone for hysteria. The calmer everyone remained the better.

"Oh my God, Meghan. What have they done to you? I should have tried to stop them. You didn't deserve this," Charlie whispered as he looked at his battered sister. Rafe watched his reactions closely.

"You did the right thing."

"What?"

"Not trying to stop them. It would have been much worse for her then."

"But she might die…"

"She won't, she can't. Where's your faith?"

"You're right. She's a fighter, always has been. Is it okay if I say a prayer?"

"Of course, you can," Rafe answered.

Ryan met Rafe's eyes, but he didn't give anything away. He'd had too many years of hiding his emotions, even if he wanted to punch something.

They listened as Charlie prayed for his sister. None of them doubted the power of prayer, they'd seen it work too many times. Rafe added his own silent prayer. Meghan needed to wake up and be okay.

A medical team was waiting as they touched down at the air force base. They loaded the women on gurneys, while Ryan accompanied them and gave them updates on their conditions. The rest of the missionary group were also brought to medical to be checked out even though they looked fine. Then they'd be flown to Ramstein Air Force Base in Germany for debriefing. After that, they'd finally get to go home.

Meghan and Miranda would have a different path. They'd be stabilized then sent to Germany for treatment. Depending on how they progressed they could be at Ramstein for a while.

Rafe didn't want to leave without seeing Meghan again, but the SEAL team was heading to Norfolk in a few hours. Their mission had been a success and it was time to go home. Normally he'd be the first one on the plane, but he didn't want to leave her again. Cam didn't look happy about leaving Miranda either.

"C'mon, bro. I know where there's a beer with your name on it." Jake put his hand on Rafe's shoulder and squeezed. "I'll make sure you have time to check on her before we take off."

"Thanks."

"She'll be fine. Look at all the shit she went through just to get here. That girl is tough."

"Yes, she is. But…"

"Give them a chance to get some fluids into her and some antibiotics. I bet she's awake and hugging her brother before we leave."

"I hope you're right."

CHAPTER 18

Voices. Afraid to open her eyes to check her surroundings, she remained still. She couldn't tell if they were speaking English or Pashto. If she could just make out what they were saying, she'd know if she was somewhere safe. The last thing she remembered was the explosions and having trouble breathing in the dust-filled room.

The gentle hum of a machine and the smell of antiseptic encouraged her to slowly open her eyes. She prayed she wasn't still tied to the chair and awaiting the next beating. The bright light hurt but brought a sigh and tears of relief. She'd been so sure she was going to die in that room.

"Praise the Lord." Turning her head toward the sound, the pain reminded her just how alive she was.

"Charlie?" Her voice cracked and sounded hoarse to her own ears.

"Hey, Meggy. Welcome back to the living."

"Charlie. Thank God you're safe. We are safe, right? I was so worried they'd figure out you were my brother and hurt you."

"Yes, we're safe. They brought us to the air force base. Your SEAL friends rescued us."

The SEALs? Rafe was there? She looked around but the only one with her was Charlie. She'd missed him, he'd probably had to go off on another mission and regret squeezed her heart.

"Are you okay?"

"I'm fine. You're the one we've been worried about. Look what they did to you. I was worried you were never going to wake up."

It was too much, too fast. The words echoed around in her head but weren't making any sense. Meghan closed her eyes to try to focus on his words, but everything was all jumbled.

A cool hand patted hers. "You have a concussion. Don't worry if things don't seem right. They will as you heal. And you need to take it slowly."

Meghan's eyes opened at the new voice.

"Give her a chance okay. She probably has a colossal headache."

"Yes, doctor. I was just so happy to see her wake up."

"Doctor…"

"Yes, Ms. Henley?"

"I know they beat me up pretty badly, but how bad is it? Will I be stuck here for long?"

214

"Besides the concussion and a fractured cheekbone, you have two broken ribs and more bruises than we could count. The swelling of your face and around your eye should go down in a day or two. It's going to be painful and hard to see until then. The good news is you will make a full recovery. Just remember it's going to take some time."

"Thank you."

"You're welcome. The more rest you get the faster you'll heal. You were unconscious for about three hours once you arrived and we're not sure how long before then. Your concussion is pretty severe."

"I understand."

"If you need anything, just push the call button. The nurse will be in to check on you shortly."

"How are you feeling?" Charlie asked as he pulled a chair to the side of her hospital bed.

"Like a human punching bag. I don't think there is a part of me that doesn't hurt but considering the alternative. I'm good."

"I'm just so glad you're alive. You were foolish to come after me."

"I needed to know you were alive. The state department wasn't telling us anything. There was no news anywhere. If it weren't for Rafe, I wouldn't have known for sure that you were taken."

"He's the big, serious looking guy?"

"Yup, that would be me."

Meghan's heart skipped a beat as she looked

beyond Charlie and met Rafe's eyes. He looked tired, but she probably looked like a one-eyed purple punching bag.

"Rafe. Oh my God, I never thought I'd see you again." Before she finished the words, he'd made it to her side and laid a gentle kiss on her forehead. It hurt but she didn't care as long as he was there with her.

"Just how well do you know him, Meggy?" Charlie asked sounding like a concerned brother.

"Ahh…"

"Yes, we do. It's a story I'll let your sister tell you when she's ready."

"Okay."

"Do you think you could give us a few minutes alone, Charlie?" Meghan asked. She loved her brother but sometimes he could be pretty dense.

"Huh? Oh… sure. I'll go check on the others. Thanks again for rescuing us, Rafe."

"You're welcome. I'm glad we got everyone out alive."

Rafe waited until the door closed behind her Charlie, then he sat on the edge of the bed and took her hand. "How's my little Spitfire? You gave me quite a scare. I thought I'd lost you."

"I thought you lost me too."

"I couldn't believe it when Tex contacted us to tell us you'd been taken. I wanted to kick his ass."

"He didn't have a choice. I was coming with or

without his help. Don't be mad at him. I'd probably be dead right now if not for him."

"Maybe. But you should have been safe in either Atlanta or DC."

"But then I wouldn't be looking into your beautiful eyes right now."

"Don't try to sweet talk me, woman."

"It won't work?" She tried to push out her lip in a seductive pout but from the look on his face she didn't pull it off.

"No, it won't. I'd take you over my knee and spank you if you weren't injured. Promise me you won't take chances like that again."

Could she make that promise? This was the job she'd worked for all of her adult life. No, she hadn't expected her family to be involved, but traveling to dangerous places to cover stories, yes. That had been the plan. But maybe it was time to make a new plan, a plan that involved one hell of a sexy SEAL. "I promise. Rafe. I was so worried I'd never see you again."

"Not going to happen, sweetheart. I told you. You're mine." He leaned down and gently kissed her lips. She tried to lift her arms, but the pain made her gasp. "I'm sorry," he said as he pulled back.

"It wasn't you. I want to hold you. Rafe, I love you. I don't know why I couldn't say it before. It didn't seem real. It was too fast, but when I thought I was going to die, all I could think about was you."

She didn't realize she was crying until a tear dripped onto her lips.

"Shhh, it's okay. You're safe now." He grabbed a tissue from the bed tray and wiped away her tears. For such a huge man he was so gentle with her. It was like a fairytale come true.

Sniffing back the rest of her tears, she tried to smile.

"You're adorable even if you are doing a great grape impersonation."

"A grape?"

"Yup. Your face is all purple and swollen."

"I'm surprised you recognized me."

"Are you kidding? I'd know you anywhere, Spitfire. I can't believe you survived all they did to you. I saw the video."

The video. She'd forgotten about that. "Oh fuck. Did they put it on the internet?"

"Afraid so. Don't worry about it. It was obvious you made it under duress."

"I hope my family doesn't see it."

"I called Tex when we got back to base, and I asked him to make it disappear. If anyone can make that happen it would be him. I also read him the riot act for sending my woman into a war zone. Mel got on the phone and almost ripped me a new one for thinking I could tell you what to do or give her husband a hard time. So, I guess we're even."

"I spoke to her, she seemed really nice. Maybe one day we can meet them?"

"Definitely. But one step at a time. You need to heal before you worry about anything else."

"I know. Do you think they'll make me stay here long?"

"Only until they're sure you're stable. It wouldn't surprise me if you were headed to Germany by tomorrow."

"Why Germany?"

"Ramstein Air Force Base. They'll be able to give you better medical attention. Then you'll be debriefed before they send you home."

"Debriefed?"

"Don't worry. It's not as bad as it sounds. They'll just want to know everything that happened. That you can remember. Don't hold anything back, because they'll find it out anyway. And don't worry about Tex, you won't get him in trouble."

"Oh good. I was worried about that. Will you be going with us?" His hand resting on her arm tensed, and she had her answer before the words left his mouth. She should have known he wouldn't be able to. He had to go where they sent him.

"I'm afraid not. We're actually leaving today. Jake, our team leader, and the captain put it off as long as possible so I could see you. I was so worried you wouldn't wake up before I had to go."

"I'll have to thank them if I ever meet them."

"You'll definitely meet the whole team."

"Can you hold me before you go?"

"Are you sure? Moving you around is going to hurt."

"Yes. I but I don't care. Who knows when we'll see each other..." The tears gathered in her eyes. What was wrong with her? She'd never been this weepy in her life.

"Sweetheart, it's okay. No tears. You'll see me again soon. I promise." He moved closer and slid his arms under her legs and shoulders and rotated her until she was lying across his lap, careful not to pull on her IV, and wrapped her in his arms. "Better now?"

"Yes." It hurt like hell, but she wasn't going to tell him. His warmth made everything a thousand times better, and even in as much pain as she was, the desire to have all of him pulsed inside her.

Her head rested in the crook of his neck and with his arms wrapped around her, she felt safe for the first time since she'd left home. Safe, and warm, and thoroughly loved. They might not have actually made love yet, but she could feel it, the truth of his love for her. They stayed that way until the nurse came in.

"You shouldn't be moving around yet, Ms. Henley."

"I know, but he's like a big heating pad and it feels good." The nurse looked between Meghan and Rafe and laughed.

"Oh yeah, I bet it does. But still, doctor's orders."

"Yes, Ma'am. I have to get going anyway."

"I'll give you a few more minutes then."

"Thank you."

"Spitfire, I have to go. I hate to leave you like this..."

"It's okay. It's what you do. I have Charlie here. Maybe they'll let him stay with me until I'm well enough to travel."

"I'm sure they will, but I'll check on it before I leave."

"See, always taking care of me."

"Always, sweetheart. We'll figure everything out when you get home. Okay?"

"Yup." She was determined not to cry again, but it was hard. Her emotions were raw, and the pain made everything worse. "I love you. Please be careful."

"I will. I'll talk to you soon. I love you, don't forget it." He laid his cheek against her then kissed her one more time before he left. Her heart ached even more than the pain in her ribs but knowing she was safe and would see him again made his leaving easier to handle.

Almost as soon as he'd left, the nurse returned. "How are you feeling?"

"Not as good as I was five minutes ago."

"I bet. That's quite a man you have there. But we'll take good care of you until you leave."

"I know you will."

The nurse made small talk as she took Meghan's vitals and then hooked up another IV bag. She appreciated that the woman was trying to take her mind off Rafe, but it wasn't working. It was as if seeing him, touching him, ignited a need that couldn't be eased without him.

"I'll be back in a bit to check on you again. Buzz if you need anything."

"I will. Thank you."

It was like a revolving door, Rafe left, the nurse came in, the nurse left, and Charlie came in. She should have been happier to see her brother considering everything, but she was tired and aching.

He sat in the chair next to the bed and looked at her for a moment without saying anything. She recognized that stare, it was just like Dad's when she was little, and he caught her doing something.

"I called Lizzie. Let her know we were both okay."

"I bet she was relieved."

"You have no idea. Apparently, you're pretty famous."

"What are you talking about?"

"The video the Taliban made of you."

"Dammit. I was hoping she'd never see it."

"It was horrible how they beat you. You should have just given in."

"You too? No, I wasn't going to give in. They would have beaten me anyway."

"Okay. Calm down. I'm not supposed to upset you. I'm sorry."

"I love you, Charlie. We were worried sick we'd never see you again. I figured if I could get an interview with the leader who'd kidnapped you, I could find out you were alive at least."

"But you were almost killed. Then Lizzie would have lost her brother and sister."

"I didn't think that part through."

"It's okay. It's over, God made sure we are all going home."

"Did you find out what happened to Miranda?"

"Yeah, your SEALs rescued her too. She got beat up pretty bad as well, but she's going to be okay. See, we were really blessed.

"Or lucky."

Charlie laughed. It was a constant debate between them, and it felt good to have something normal even if it only lasted for a few moments.

"Oh, I almost forgot. Rafe left this for you. I think he wrote it when he thought he'd have to leave before you woke up."

The envelope was addressed to her, his handwriting was bold as she'd expected. There was nothing meek about that man. She contemplated waiting until she was alone to read it but couldn't resist. Tearing open the envelope, she pulled out a single sheet of paper.

Spitfire,

I am so glad you're okay. You are one of the bravest women I know but you could have been killed. I could have lost you forever.

Please follow the doctor's orders and get well. I'll see you when you get back home. Promise me you won't take any more chances.

I love you and when you're better I'll show you just how much. I will talk to you soon, sweetheart.

Yours,

Rafe

She re-read it twice more before she tucked it back into the envelope.

"Everything okay?" Charlie asked.

"Yes, it's perfect."

CHAPTER 19

It had been two months since Rafe had seen her. As usual with the life of a special operator, they'd been sent on a mission, and as usual, the timing sucked. They'd left the day after she'd gotten back to Atlanta with Charlie.

He'd planned on giving her a few days at home with her family, then show up and bring her to his apartment to finish her recovery. He'd even redecorated his apartment to make it feel less like a bachelor pad. But as most of his long term plans, they got blown out of the water, such was the life of a frogman.

Before he'd left, he'd given Tex a call. After thinking about everything Meghan had said about her going with or without his help it would be wrong to be pissed at Tex. Instead, he owed him a huge debt that he'd kept her as safe as possible.

"Hey, Tex."

"Rafe, how's it going? Are you ready to kick my ass now?"

"I was tempted. But Meghan saved you."

"She did?"

"Yeah. The little Spitfire made it clear she would have gone even if you hadn't helped her. And because of you, she's alive now. So how could I be upset? You saved her as much as we did."

"I don't know about that. But I'm glad you understood. I was afraid if I said no, she'd take off and really get into trouble. Not that she didn't anyway."

"Exactly. And the tracking on her phone? Pure genius."

"Yeah, well I've done that for a few others when their wives were in trouble."

"I was wondering. Could you do it again? Put a tracker on her phone? She needs a new one and I was hoping you could add it. Not that I am trying to be a stalker, I just want to make sure there's no backlash."

"Normally I'd say no. But you're right. Azfaar is still in the wind and even more dangerous after you took out his brother. So, I'll do it."

"Can you program my number in too? I want to make sure she has it even if I can't answer when we're on missions."

"No problem."

"Also, when she's feeling better, we're going to

come and visit if that's okay. She really wants to thank you and meet Mel."

"That sounds great. You're welcome anytime. I know Mel would love to meet her too."

"Great. Thanks again. Give Mel my love."

Once she'd received the phone, they'd spoken a lot and thankfully Lizzie helped him convince her to stay in Atlanta until he returned. Since he hadn't known how long he'd be gone it wasn't an easy sell. But having his Spitfire back made it worth all the debates and pleading.

The Black Eagle team was sent to Syria to locate the chemist responsible for the manufacture of a new chemical compound the Russians were trying to weaponize. They'd had intel that he would be in Aleppo but when they'd arrived his lab was destroyed and there was no sign of him.

They'd spent the following week tracking down every lead they could get before they were told to come home. Rafe knew it wouldn't be the last they heard of Dr. Yasser Abaza. But now he had a week of leave and a woman to fetch.

After he got back to the apartment, he showered, changed and sent Meghan a text message.

How's my Spitfire? Feeling better? I sure hope so, because I'm back and I can't wait to see you.

While he waited for her response, he went through the refrigerator and tossed the spoiled milk and leftovers. He'd have to get some food when they got back. He realized he didn't even know how she took her coffee, or if she even drank coffee. Fuck a duck, he was head over heels for a woman and he didn't know anything personal about her.

Welcome home, big guy. I have a surprise for you. A surprise? He'd made her promise to stay in Atlanta, she shouldn't have been able to get into any trouble with Lizzie watching over her.

Should I be worried?

No. It's a good surprise. I'm already in Norfolk. You don't have to go to Atlanta to get me. Isn't that great?

What happened to staying in Atlanta until I got back?

Really? You're going to give me grief now? I saved you an eight hour drive each way.

He wanted to be mad, he really did. But he missed her like crazy and couldn't wait to hold her in his arms. So, no he wasn't going to give her grief. As he was typing his reply, his phone rang and without looking he knew it was Meghan.

"No, I'm not going to give you grief."

"Good thing. I wanted more time with you. Chrissy came to visit, and I drove back with her. No big deal. Now are you going to come and get me, or should we drive over?"

"Give me her address and I'll be right there."

The drive to Chrissy's condo should have taken about ten minutes, but every freaking light turned red as he approached it. It was like his timing was off. Nerves, something he didn't usually experience. He had no doubt about his feelings for her, but he couldn't help the niggling little worry that maybe she didn't feel the same way.

Everything had happened so quickly, and with so much fear and turmoil, maybe she just had that hero complex thing. It would rip him to shreds, but he'd let her go. Her happiness was the only thing that mattered. He'd accepted the fact that he'd be alone, he could get to that place again. As long as Meghan was safe and happy.

As he pulled into the parking spot, the door of the condo opened. She must have been watching for him and he knew he had a shit eating grin on his face. He got out of the car as she ran outside and jumped into his arms.

"Whoa, you're going to hurt yourself."

"I don't care. I missed you so much. I was starting to think you were trying to avoid me."

"Never." He pulled her closer and kissed her. He longed for so much more, but the parking lot was not the place. "I missed you too, Spitfire. I'm glad you don't look like a grape anymore." She'd healed well. There were only slight traces of bruising around her right eye. He hoped the rest of her had healed as well.

"Damn straight. I'm just about back to normal. Now, aren't you glad I came to Norfolk?"

"Yes and no. But mostly yes." Rafe kissed her again and gently stood her on the ground. "Should we go inside and hang out for a bit with Chrissy?"

"It would be nice, but I think she'll understand if we don't stay," Meghan said and waggled her eyebrows. "We can invite her to come for dinner before I leave."

"That works for me. Where's your bag?"

"By the front door. I'll go grab it."

"No, you won't. I'll get it and you can introduce me to Chrissy."

Rafe had heard plenty about Meghan's best friend and he had formed an idea of what she'd be like. He couldn't have been more wrong. Chrissy Stillwell was the complete opposite of his spitfire—tall, short blonde hair, and big brown eyes.

"Rafe, nice to meet you finally," Chrissy said as she shook his hand.

"It's good to meet you as well. Thank you for bringing Meghan to Norfolk."

Chrissy laughed. "Like I had a choice. Oh my God, she would have driven me batshit crazy if I hadn't brought her." When Rafe glanced at Meghan, her cheeks were tinged pink.

"What? I haven't seen you in two months. I didn't want to wait extra time for you to come and get me at my sister's. This is so much better."

It was better, and to say anything else would make him a hypocrite. "You win. But next time you make me a promise you'd better keep it."

"Yes, big bad Navy SEAL, sir," she answered then stuck her tongue out. Oh yeah, she was going to get it once they were alone.

Chrissy burst out laughing. "Good luck, Rafe. She's all yours now. Call if you need me to come to the rescue."

"Thanks, but I think we'll be fine. She's one little bitty spitfire and I can just pick her up and put her on a shelf if she gets out of hand," Rafe said with a wink. The expression on Meghan's face was priceless and he chuckled.

"Come on, trouble maker. You need to rest. Thank you again, Chrissy."

"Anytime." She hugged Meghan and whispered something in her ear that made her giggle. It was so good to see her laughing and smiling.

"I DON'T HAVE a lot of food in the apartment. Do you want to stop at the store on the way home?"

"I have a bag of things I picked up with Chrissy yesterday. I think we can wait. I didn't know if you drank coffee or how you took it if you did, so I bought all of it. I need my coffee in the morning or I'm a bear."

Rafe laughed. "A bear huh? I was thinking the same thing before I came to get you. I need my coffee in the morning too. But I wasn't sure if you drank it."

"If I could I'd take it by IV, but I usually add some cream and sugar. How about you?"

"Black. The stronger the better. Jake warns

everyone when I make the coffee at work that it's strong enough to wake the neighbors."

She giggled. "Jake is in charge of your team, right?"

"Yeah. You'll probably meet them all sometime this week."

"Maybe we can have a small party. Invite your team and Chrissy."

"Let's see how you're feeling first."

"Rafe, I swear. I'm fine. Really. The ribs hardly hurt at all. The worst part was my face and that is better now."

"We'll talk about it tomorrow. Okay?"

"Yeah. I know I'm rambling. I might just be a tad bit nervous."

"Why, sweetheart?"

"Umm, you, me, it's been kind of a whirlwind thing. It was hard for me to accept it, I'm too cynical. My whole world is about facts. At least, it was until we met. Then you blew that out of the water."

Rafe pulled the car over to the curb. No way was he going to wait until he got her to the apartment to discuss this. "Does that mean you've changed your mind about us?

"No, not only no, but fuck no. Do you think I would have been so excited to see you, or even gotten in the car with you if I had? I just want you to understand that this is a huge leap for me. But I don't want to take back even one moment, even if there were times, I asked myself 'what the fuck'."

"This isn't exactly where I wanted to have this conversation, but we're all about adapt and improvise." He took her hand and turned it palm up then kissed it. "Meghan, you are it for me. I knew it almost as soon as I looked into your eyes. I will never want anyone else. I was resigned to never finding the right woman, and then there you were."

Tears glistened in her eyes. "I feel the same way. I can't imagine my life without you. I don't know what I did to deserve you, but I will be thankful for the rest of my life that we were stuck in that airport."

Gently he pulled her close and kissed her with all the pent up emotions he'd held back for so long. Sweeping her mouth with his tongue, learning her taste, her feel. Her low moan reminded him where they were, and he pulled back.

"I'm sorry. I need to get you home where I can erase any residual doubts you might have. I've been dreaming about this for weeks."

The worry he'd been holding onto floated away like a feather in the breeze. They were so alike and so different at the same time. But he was no longer concerned that her feelings for him weren't real. What he'd told her was true, she was everything he'd ever wanted and so much more. He couldn't wait to get her alone so he could show her.

"How much further?"

"Not long. I hope you like it."

"I will."

"How can you know that?"

"Because you live there. It's all that's important."

"I'm going to have to watch out for those words of yours. I keep forgetting you're a writer."

Meghan laughed. "You don't have to worry. Besides, I'm not sure I'm going back to the paper. I'm trying to decide what to do with my future."

"I figured they'd give you a promotion after all you'd been through."

"They offered to let me go on assignments and cover hard news instead of the society page. But I'm not sure that's what I want anymore."

From the tone of her voice, he knew there was more going on. But again, the car wasn't the place to talk about it. They had at least a week together, if he was lucky, and maybe he'd be able to stretch it to two. They'd have time to talk about all the little things they needed to. Just not tonight. Tonight, he had other plans.

CHAPTER 20

After following Rafe into his apartment, Meghan was impressed and more than a little surprised. She'd imagined a bachelor pad, with a huge TV, maybe one or two chairs, and nothing on the walls. But it was the complete opposite, except for the huge TV. But if it hadn't been there, she'd have been worried, as in 'where is the real Rafe and what did they do with him' worried.

"Nice place and not at all what I expected."

"I'm glad you like it. But I'll be honest, I kind of gave it an overhaul after you agreed to come."

"You mean it wasn't always like this?" she asked with a smile. It made more sense now.

"Not exactly. Let me show you around. The kitchen is through here," he said as he showed her the kitchen area with a breakfast nook.

"Perfect for morning coffee."

"Exactly. Although I usually have mine as I'm

running out the door." Meghan's heart skipped a beat when he took her hand and lead her down the hallway. "This is the main bathroom, and closest to the second bedroom. That's in here." He stopped and looked at her as he opened the door. It was the first time she could remember him looking at all unsure of himself.

"You're welcome to sleep in here, but I'd rather you sleep with me." His eyes were so intensely focused on her she thought he'd be able to see right into her brain.

"I'd rather I sleep with you too." As soon as the words left her lips, her world tilted. He picked her up and carried her down the hall to the last door like he was afraid she would change her mind.

"Whoa, big guy. Put me down. I am more than capable of moving on my own."

"I know, but I love carrying you. Besides, it's faster this way."

Meghan laughed at how gently he placed her on the bed after the way he'd swung her into his arms in the hallway. The thrill of the moment. Then he probably remembered her broken ribs.

"I've waited my whole life to have you in my arms, in my bed, in my heart."

She understood the feeling. They'd only known each other for a couple of months, and most of that time had been spent apart, but she'd never felt closer to another human being in her life. He was the missing part of her heart, the reason why no one had ever swept her off her feet. One of these days, she was going to have to send Delta Airlines a thank you for canceling their flight.

Rafe pulled off his shirt and kicked off his shoes then stretched out next to her on the bed. "When I found you in the compound, I wondered if I'd ever be able to look into your big green eyes again. I thought I'd lost you." As he spoke, he leaned his forehead against hers and she felt him shudder.

"When they dragged me out of that jeep in the desert, I thought the same thing. Then when they didn't bring me to Azfaar and threw me in the cell, I figured my life was over."

"Tex had that tracker in your phone so he knew pretty much where you were all the time. And he was able to let us know about where you were. You were smart to keep it with you for as long as you did. It's what saved his ass for letting you go over there."

"I told you..." She didn't have a chance to tell him for the fifteen millionth time that she'd have gone with or without Tex's help. He took possession of her mouth. His tongue swept in and stole her words and her breath. Straddling her body, he balanced on his arms hands instead of leaning on her. But that wasn't close enough. Her need for him was so intense she didn't care if her ribs cracked all over again.

Reaching around his waist, she tried to pull him against her, but he resisted, and deepened the kiss until her toes curled. When she was breathless and dazed, he pulled away and gave her the sexiest smile she'd ever seen. If the kiss hadn't already lit her on fire that grin would have.

"Is there something you want, my little Spitfire?"

"Yes, dammit. Are you going to make me beg?"

"I should after what you did, but I'd be torturing both of us."

"So, big guy, what are you waiting for?"

"Are you sure you want this?"

"Hell, yes. Now, make love to me. Pretty please." Batting her eyelashes, she tried to look alluring.

Rafe didn't say a word, didn't have to. He stood up opened the bedside table and pulled out a box of condoms. A whole box. His eyes burned with passion and her body answered. Then he removed his jeans, slowly, so she could get a good look at all of him. She'd dreamed about this moment, imagined what he'd look like, but nothing prepared her for the reality.

Over six foot of sheer muscle, chiseled to perfection, and multiple scars proving his warrior status. Licking her lips, she tried to speak but her words caught in her throat. But he read her mind.

"You've got way too much on." Hell yeah she did. Sitting up, she pulled her t-shirt over her head and tossed it onto the floor. For a few heartbeats she was self-conscious about her body, not the curves, she was proud of those, but the bruises that still covered her stomach and chest. She didn't want those to be a distraction, and it had been another reason she'd asked Chrissy to take her shopping for some sexy lingerie. Seeing his look of appreciation, made it more than worth all the money she'd spent.

Kneeling, she undid the button and lowered the zipper on her jeans. As she shimmied out of them, she held her breath as she waited for his reaction. It was the first time he'd be able to see the remnants of her captivity, and she was sure he'd noticed her hesitation.

Climbing back onto the bed he slid down next to her and pulled her into his arms. "You are absolutely the most gorgeous woman I've ever seen."

"But…"

"No buts. You are the most beautiful woman in the world from the top of your head of black locks to the tiny soles of your feet. I love all of you, every curve, every dimple, and yes, every bruise. Although I hate knowing how you suffered. Never think for one moment that you're not perfect and always will be, even when we're old and wrinkly."

Once again, he'd made tears glisten in her eyes. What woman wouldn't want their man to believe they were beautiful? But she was a realist, and knew she was far from it, but that he believed it was all that mattered.

He brushed his thumb under her eyes and caught a tear before it slipped down her cheek. "No more tears, sweetheart." Leaning down, he kissed each eyelid, her cheeks, the tip of her nose, and then her lips reigniting the fire in both of them.

"Please, Rafe, I need you." He didn't answer but continued to kiss and lick his way down her body. He kissed every bruise and took extra care not to put any pressure on her ribs. Then he spread her legs and the first touch of his tongue on her clit, almost sent her off the bed. Her fingers clenched in the bedding, as she pushed against him, wanting more. When he took her clit into his mouth and sucked, she arched up off the bed and shuddered as the orgasm shook her to her core.

He didn't give her a chance to catch her breath. Already licking and sucking up her juices before sliding a finger inside. Slowly he thrust in and out until her muscles tensed and every nerve in her body burned with desire. Then she came apart into a million little pieces of pleasure.

She'd never experienced anything like the mind-numbing orgasm he'd given her. And she wanted more, but not this way.

"I need you."

"I know, sweetheart." He grabbed a condom and slid it on. "I'll go slow. If anything hurts tell me and I'll stop. Promise."

"I promise." Her breath caught as the tip of his cock rubbed against her clit and then pushed against her opening. It was for her, she knew it, but it was too slow. She needed him inside, to fill her.

Grabbing his shoulders, she arched her back, pushing him further inside.

"Easy, I don't want to hurt you."

"You won't. I want all of you." And she arched again, pulling more of him into her. Clenching her muscles to hold him inside.

He groaned and buried himself to the hilt. She'd never been so full. He stilled, giving her a chance to get used to his size then pulled most of the way out before pushing back in, faster and harder with each thrust.

It was too much, but not enough, and she wrapped her legs around his waist. Holding him closer, burning brighter and harder until the sun exploded around them as he yelled her name.

Satiated, unable to move, she felt like a puddle of pure happiness. He dropped his forehead to hers and kissed her before sliding to her side and pulling her against him.

"That was…"

"Incredible? Amazing? Mind-blowing?"

Rafe laughed. "I was going to say what true love must feel like. But they all work too." He'd done it again, took her breath away, this time with his words.

"You're amazing, Rafe. Just when I think I can't love you anymore you say something like that."

"I hope I can always make you feel that way."

"I love you with all my heart. You've rocked my world in every way possible."

"You've done the same for me. Given me so much more than I can explain."

She cuddled closer and her fingers traced the scars on his chest. Someday she'd ask about them, but not tonight.

A yawn escaped and she tried to hide it against his side, but his super SEAL powers heard it.

"You need to rest."

"I don't want to."

"I'll be here when you wake up. I promise."

She didn't remember falling asleep, but when she opened her eyes again, the sun was shining in through the window. Rafe's arm was tucked around her and her head was still lying on his chest. Afraid to move, worried that she'd wake him, she stayed where she was and listened to his even breathing and his heartbeat. Strong, just like him.

Meghan had thought long and hard about what she'd do next with her life, and whether she wanted to go back to the paper and take the promotion, she'd worked so hard to get. But that would mean staying in Washington, DC when Rafe needed to be in Norfolk. She'd talked to Lizzie and Chrissy about it and they told her to follow her instincts.

Over the last few weeks, she'd made lists of pros and cons, trying to make her decision. Wondering if she gave up her earlier dream if it would come back to haunt her later. But then she reminded herself, she didn't have to give it up. She could still write, cover stories, just do it on her own, on a blog, or website, or just put out books. As Lizzie kept reminding her, she had a great one to start with. But it wasn't until Rafe texted that he was coming home and couldn't wait to see her that she finally made her decision.

"I'm awake, you don't have to pretend you're still sleeping." His rough and sexy morning voice sent a shiver down her spine. She was sore from last night, but she was still tempted to straddle him and see how he liked morning sex.

"Morning, big guy. You make a wonderful pillow." The rumble of his laughter made her smile.

"I'm glad you enjoyed it. How are you? Sore?"

"I'm good."

"Meghan..."

"Okay, maybe a little sore but in a wonderful way."

"Better. I always want the truth, sweetheart, good or bad. We'll always get through it together whatever it is."

"I promise, truth always. And since we're being truthful, I really need to use the bathroom followed by a cup of coffee."

Rafe chuckled. "Your wish is my command. I'll go start the coffee."

Grabbing a shower while she was in the bathroom, she met him in the kitchen in one of his Navy t-shirts she'd stolen from one of his drawers.

He had the coffee poured and ready when she walked in and was already sitting in the nook watching the birds through the window. Adding the cream and sugar to her mug, she went to sit at the table when he pulled her onto his lap.

"Good morning, Spitfire. You look good enough to eat."

"Umm, I think we went there already."

"I guess we did," Rafe said with a chuckle. She loved this side of him, so lighthearted. His chiseled features looked softer somehow.

In the shower, she'd thought about how to bring it up, about her job, their future, but she was also still a little afraid that just because he loved her didn't mean they both wanted the same thing.

Cuddled against him while sipping her coffee, was like something out of one of her dreams. But it also made her hesitate about bringing up the future.

"What's wrong? I felt you get tense."

"Nothing is wrong. I just…"

"Remember, Spitfire, you can tell me anything. I'm yours, you're mine. It's how it works."

Taking his words to heart, she put her mug down on the table. "Remember when you asked me about my job?"

"Yeah."

"I turned down the promotion. Actually, I quit." She waited a few seconds to see his response, but he was perfectly still, calm, just waiting for her to continue. "I'm going to write a book about what happened in Afghanistan. I thought I might be able to do it in Norfolk..." Her voice trailed off. He was quiet at first, and her old insecurities crept back in, then he tilted her chin up and she met his eyes.

"Does that mean you'll move in with me? Or do I have to compete with Chrissy?"

"You. You. Always you. I was praying you'd be okay with this. Chrissy was my backup plan although she didn't know it. I haven't told anyone. I wanted to make sure you'd be okay with this first."

"I'm better than okay. I'm thrilled. I'd been wondering how we were going to make this work with you in DC. I figured we'd be doing a lot of driving back and forth. But are you sure? I know journalism was your dream."

"It was, but after everything that happened, I realized that it wasn't what I really wanted, and I will still write. I figure I could get a job on a local paper or start a blog or something."

"I'll support whatever you decide. I just hope whatever it is means we can stay together."

"Always, Rafe. Always."

EPILOGUE

The next day, Rafe drove them up to DC to clean out Meghan's apartment. It was only a little furnished studio, and there wasn't that much stuff to pack up. Mostly pictures and books. When they were finished, she dropped the keys off with the landlord and then they headed home. Meghan liked the sound of that. Her apartment had never felt like home, just a place to stay on the way to somewhere else. And now she had her somewhere else.

After going back and forth about it, they decided to have a small party on Friday. Rafe invited his team, including Captain Knox, and Meghan invited Chrissy. It would be pizza and beer and give Meghan a chance to thank Rafe's team for everything they did.

~

"Do I look all right?"

"Sweetheart, you're beautiful."

"You're not even looking at me."

"But you're always beautiful. Even when you look like a grape." It was a good thing he ducked or the pillow she'd tossed would have hit him in the face. "Hey, was that necessary?"

"Yes. It was. I'm serious. I'm nervous about meeting your team. I want to make the right impression."

"You already did."

"How is that possible?"

"Because you make me happy. That's enough for them."

"Dammit, Rafe. I love you."

"Just don't throw any more pillows." They were both still laughing when the doorbell rang. Chrissy was the first to arrive followed by Ryan and Murph. Rafe did the introductions and Meghan handed out the beers.

Captain Knox and Jake were next, the only one missing was Cam. They were just about to start serving the pizza figuring something held him up when the doorbell rang.

"Hey, Cam. I was starting to think you were going to stand us up."

"Nope, just had to make a side trip. I hope you don't mind that I brought a date."

"Halo?"

"Nope, me." Miranda Stanhope stepped out

from behind Cam. Rafe shouldn't have been surprised considering how they'd been during her rescue, and he couldn't have been happier. He hoped Cam realized that dating a senator's daughter was going to be a little more complicated than the women he usually dated.

"It's great to see you, Miranda. I'm glad you're doing well. C'mon in. Everyone else is already here."

Rafe rejoined Meghan where she sat on the couch. Wrapping his arm around her, he pulled her close and listened to all the bits of conversations going on around them. Life was good, he had his friends and the woman he loved by his side. It just didn't get better than that.

The End

ABOUT THE AUTHOR

Lynne St. James is the author of eighteen books in romantic suspense, contemporary and new adult romance. She lives in the mostly sunny state of Florida with her husband, an eighty-five-pound, fluffy, Dalmatian-mutt horse-dog, a small Yorkie-poo, and an orange tabby named Pumpkin who rules them all.

When Lynne's not writing stories about second chances and conquering adversity with happily ever afters, she's drinking coffee, and reading or crocheting.

Where to find Lynne:

Email: lynne@lynnestjames.com
Amazon: https://amzn.to/2sgdUTe
BookBub:
https://www.bookbub.com/authors/lynne-st-james
Facebook:
https://www.facebook.com/authorLynneStJames
Website: http://lynnestjames.com
Instagram:
https://www.instagram.com/lynnestjames/

Pinterest:
https://www.pinterest.com/lynnestjames5

VIP   Newsletter   sign-up:
http://eepurl.com/bT99Fj

- facebook.com/authorLynneStJames
- instagram.com/lynnestjames
- pinterest.com/lynnestjames5
- bookbub.com/authors/lynne-st-james

BOOKS BY LYNNE ST. JAMES

Beyond Valor

A Soldier's Gift

A Soldier's Forever

A Soldier's Triumph

A Soldier's Protection

A Soldier's Pledge

A Soldier's Destiny (Previously Guarding Aurora), (re-release soon)

A Soldier's Temptation (Previously Protecting Ariana), (re-release soon)

A Soldier's Homecoming (TBD)

A Soldier's Redemption (TBD)

Black Eagle Team

SEAL's Spitfire

Raining Chaos

Taming Chaos

Seducing Wrath

Music Under the Mistletoe - A Raining Chaos Christmas (novella)

Tempting Flame

<u>Anamchara</u>

Embracing Her Desires

Embracing Her Surrender

Embracing Her Love

<u>The Vampires of Eternity</u>

Twice Bitten Not Shy

Twice Bitten to Paradise

Twice Bitten and Bewitched

Want to be one of the first to learn about Lynne St. James's new releases? Sign up for her newsletter filled with exclusive VIP news and contests!
http://eepurl.com/bT99Fj

As you know, this book included at least one character from Susan Stoker's books. To check out more, see below.

SEAL of Protection: Legacy Series
Securing Caite
Securing Brenae (novella) (April 2019)
Securing Sidney (May 2019)
Securing Piper (Sept 2019)
Securing Zoey (TBA)
Securing Avery (TBA)
Securing Kalee (TBA)

Delta Force Heroes Series
Rescuing Rayne (FREE!)
Rescuing Aimee (novella)
Rescuing Emily
Rescuing Harley
Marrying Emily
Rescuing Kassie
Rescuing Bryn
Rescuing Casey
Rescuing Sadie
Rescuing Wendy
Rescuing Mary
Rescuing Macie (April 2019)

Badge of Honor: Texas Heroes Series
Justice for Mackenzie (FREE!)

Justice for Mickie
Justice for Corrie
Justice for Laine (novella)
Shelter for Elizabeth
Justice for Boone
Shelter for Adeline
Shelter for Sophie
Justice for Erin
Justice for Milena
Shelter for Blythe
Justice for Hope
Shelter for Quinn
Shelter for Koren (July 2019)
Shelter for Penelope (Oct 2019)

SEAL of Protection Series

Protecting Caroline (FREE!)
Protecting Alabama
Protecting Fiona
Marrying Caroline (novella)
Protecting Summer
Protecting Cheyenne
Protecting Jessyka
Protecting Julie (novella)
Protecting Melody
Protecting the Future
Protecting Kiera (novella)
Protecting Dakota

New York Times, USA Today and *Wall Street Journal*

Bestselling Author Susan Stoker has a heart as big as the state of Tennessee where she lives, but this all American girl has also spent the last fourteen years living in Missouri, California, Colorado, Indiana, and Texas. She's married to a retired Army man who now gets to follow *her* around the country.

She debuted her first series in 2014 and quickly followed that up with the SEAL of Protection Series, which solidified her love of writing and creating stories readers can get lost in.

If you enjoyed this book, or any book, please consider leaving a review. It's appreciated by authors more than you'll know.

www.stokeraces.com

www.AcesPress.com

susan@stokeraces.com

*There are many more books in this fan fiction world
than listed here, for an up-to-date list go to
www.AcesPress.com*

*You can also visit our Amazon page at:
http://www.amazon.com/author/operationalpha*

Special Forces: Operation Alpha World
Denise Agnew: Dangerous to Hold
Shauna Allen: Awakening Aubrey
Shauna Allen: Defending Danielle
Shauna Allen: Rescuing Rebekah
Shauna Allen: Saving Scarlett
Shauna Allen: Saving Grace
Brynne Asher: Blackburn
Jennifer Becker: Hiding Catherine
Julia Bright: Saving Lorelei
Julia Bright: Rescuing Amy
Victoria Bright: Surviving Savage
Victoria Bright: Going Ghost
Victoria Bright: Jostling Joker
Cara Carnes: Protecting Mari
Kendra Mei Chailyn: Beast
Kendra Mei Chailyn: Barbie
Kendra Mei Chailyn : Pitbull
Melissa Kay Clarke: Rescuing Annabeth
Melissa Kay Clarke: Safeguarding Miley
Samantha A. Cole: Handling Haven
Samantha A. Cole: Cheating the Devil

Sue Coletta: Hacked

Melissa Combs: Gallant

KaLyn Cooper: Rescuing Melina

Liz Crowe: Marking Mariah

Jordan Dane: Redemption for Avery

Jordan Dane: Fiona's Salvation

Riley Edwards: Protecting Olivia

Riley Edwards: Redeeming Violet

Riley Edwards, Recovering Ivy

Nicole Flockton: Protecting Maria

Nicole Flockton: Guarding Erin

Nicole Flockton: Guarding Suzie

Nicole Flockton: Guarding Brielle

Casey Hagen: Shielding Nebraska

Casey Hagen: Shielding Harlow

Casey Hagen: Shielding Josie

Casey Hagen: Shielding Blair

Desiree Holt: Protecting Maddie

Kathy Ivan: Saving Sarah

Kathy Ivan: Saving Savannah

Kathy Ivan: Saving Stephanie

Jesse Jacobson: Protecting Honor

Jesse Jacobson: Fighting for Honor

Jesse Jacobson: Defending Honor

Jesse Jacobson: Summer Breeze

Silver James: Rescue Moon

Silver James: SEAL Moon

Silver James: Assassin's Moon

Silver James: Under the Assassin's Moon

Becca Jameson: Saving Sofia

Kate Kinsley: Protecting Ava
Heather Long: Securing Arizona
Heather Long: Guarding Gertrude
Heather Long: Protecting Pilar
Heather Long: Covering Coco
Gennita Low: No Protection
Kirsten Lynn: Joining Forces for Jesse
Margaret Madigan: Bang for the Buck
Margaret Madigan: Buck the System
Margaret Madigan: Jungle Buck
Margaret Madigan: December Chill
Rachel McNeely: The SEAL's Surprise Baby
Rachel McNeely: The SEAL's Surprise Bride
Rachel McNeely: The SEAL's Surprise Twin
KD Michaels: Saving Laura
KD Michaels: Protecting Shane
KD Michaels: Avenging Angels
Wren Michaels: The Fox & The Hound
Wren Michaels: The Fox & The Hound 2
Wren Michaels: Shadow of Doubt
Wren Michaels: Shift of Fate
Wren Michaels: Steeling His Heart
Kat Mizera: Protecting Bobbi
Mary B Moore: Force Protection
LeTeisha Newton: Protecting Butterfly
LeTeisha Newton: Protecting Goddess
LeTeisha Newton: Protecting Vixen
LeTeisha Newton: Protecting Heartbeat
MJ Nightingale: Protecting Beauty
MJ Nightingale: Betting on Benny

MJ Nightingale: Protecting Secrets
Sarah O'Rourke: Saving Liberty
Debra Parmley: Protecting Pippa
Lainey Reese: Protecting New York
Jenika Snow: Protecting Lily
Jen Talty: Burning Desire
Jen Talty: Burning Kiss
Jen Talty: Burning Skies
Jen Talty: Burning Lies
Jen Talty: Burning Heart
Megan Vernon: Protecting Us
Megan Vernon: Protecting Earth

Fire and Police: Operation Alpha World
Freya Barker: Burning for Autumn
KaLyn Cooper: Justice for Gwen
Aspen Drake: Sheltering Emma
Barb Han: Kace
Reina Torres: Justice for Sloane
Stacey Wilk: Stage Fright

Made in the USA
Monee, IL
31 March 2021